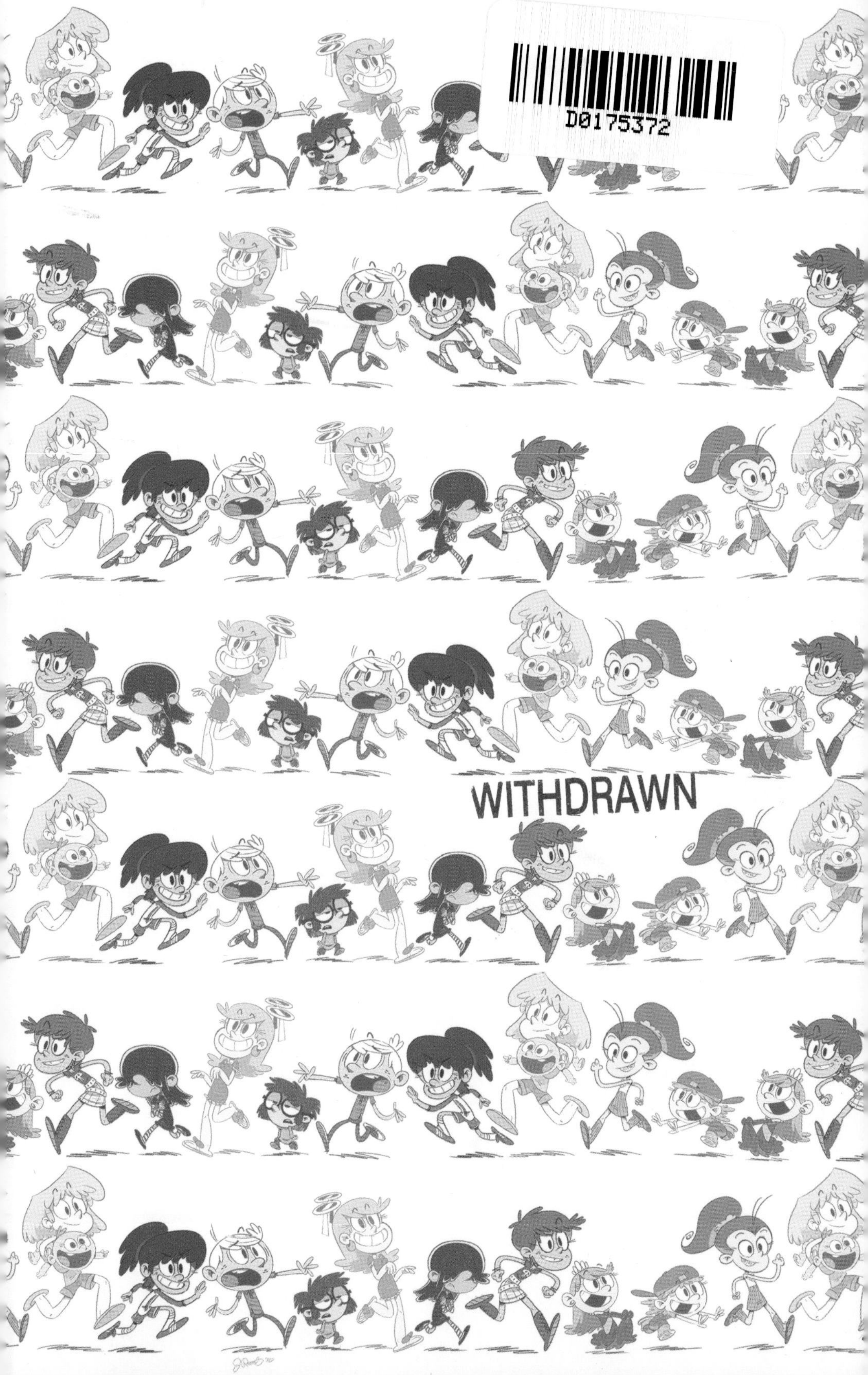

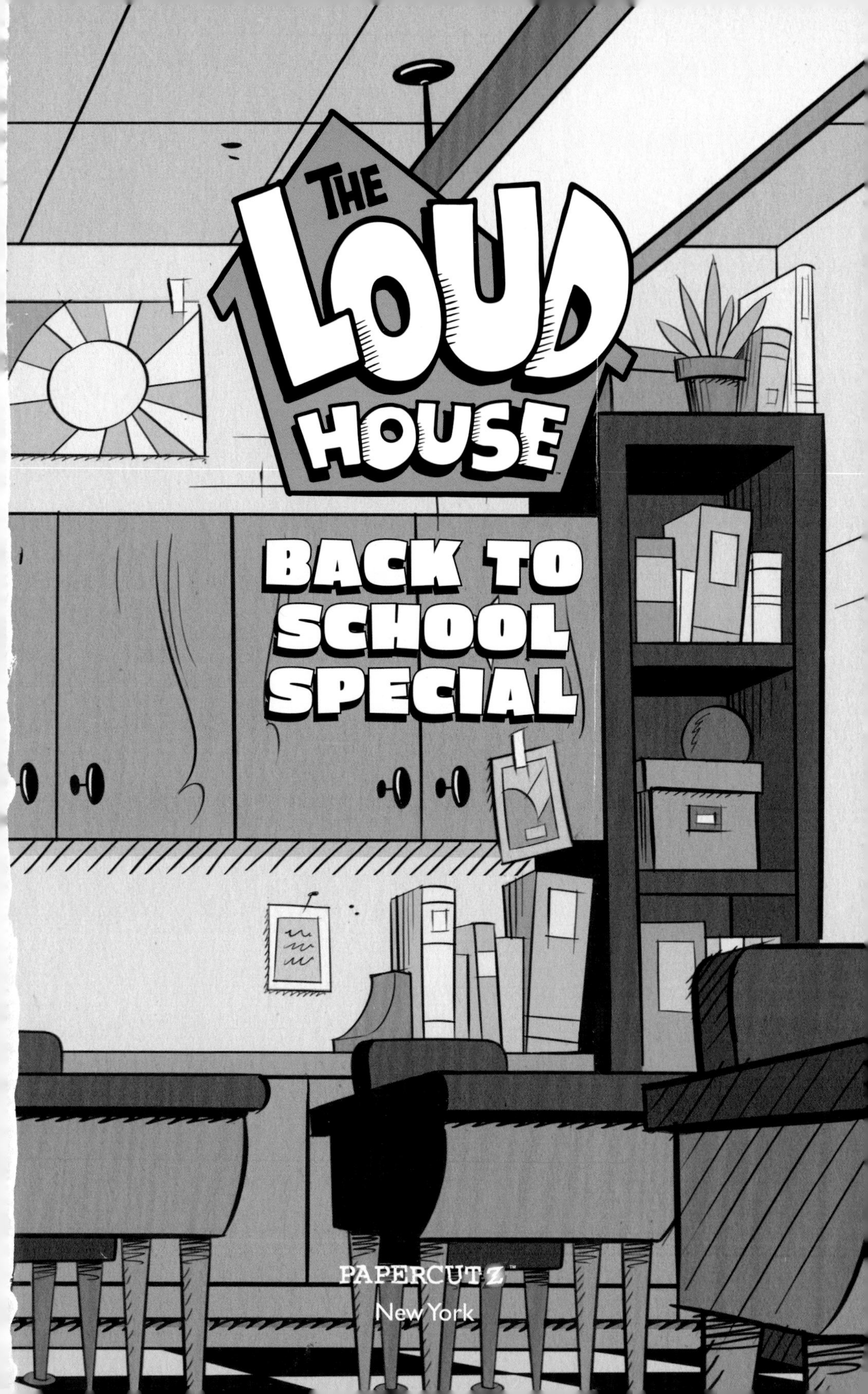

THE LOUD HOUSE

BACK TO SCHOOL SPECIAL

PAPERCUTZ™
New York

MORE GREAT GRAPHIC NOVEL SERIES AVAILABLE FROM

PAPERCUTZ™

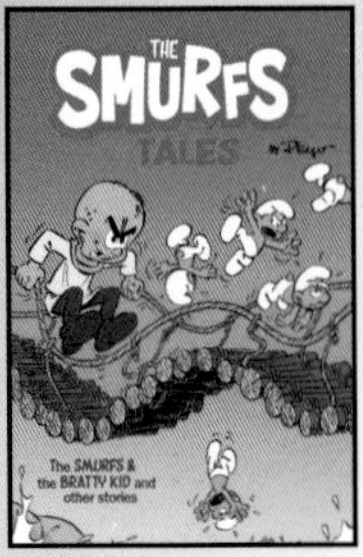
THE SMURFS TALES

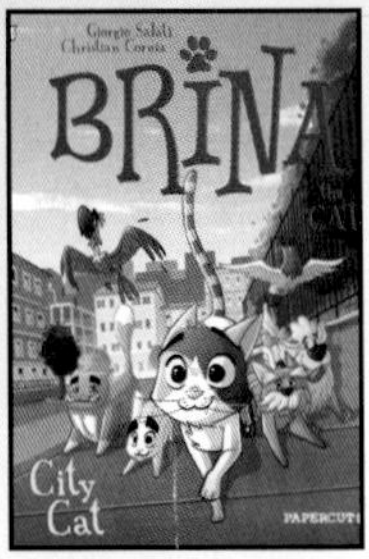
BRINA THE CAT

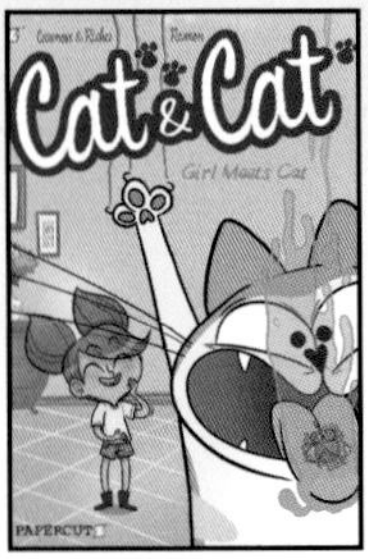
CAT & CAT

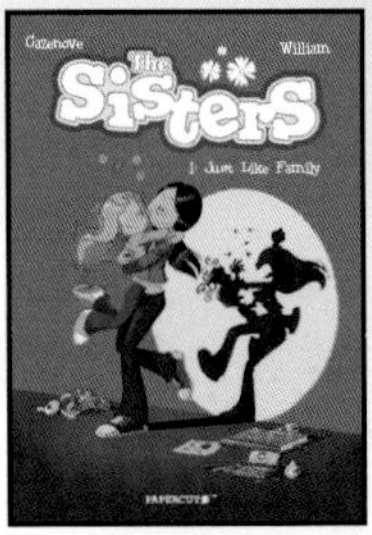
THE SISTERS

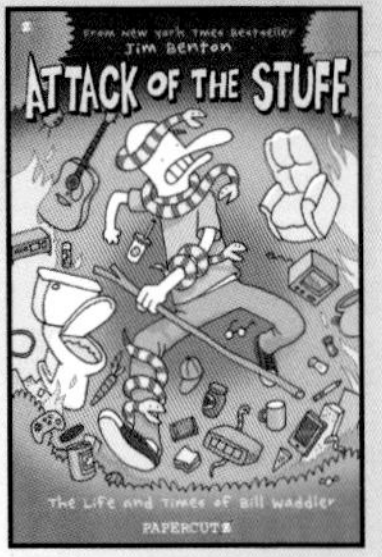
ATTACK OF THE STUFF

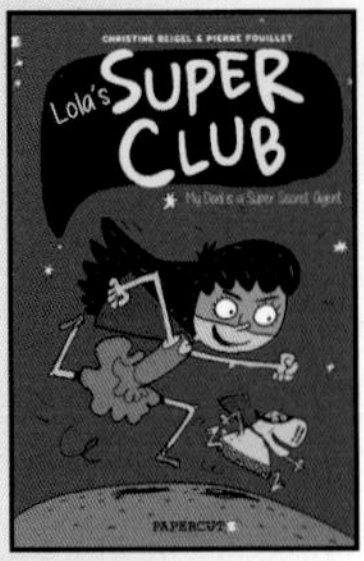
LOLA'S SUPER CLUB

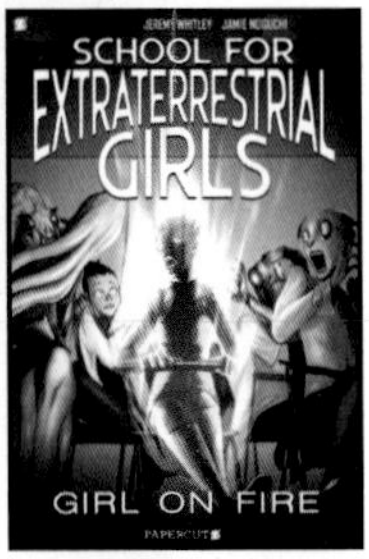
SCHOOL FOR EXTRATERRESTRIAL GIRLS

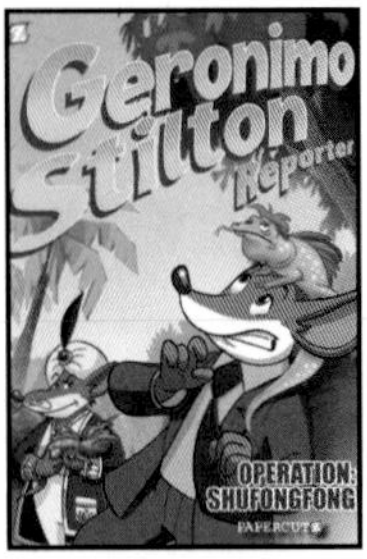
GERONIMO STILTON REPORTER

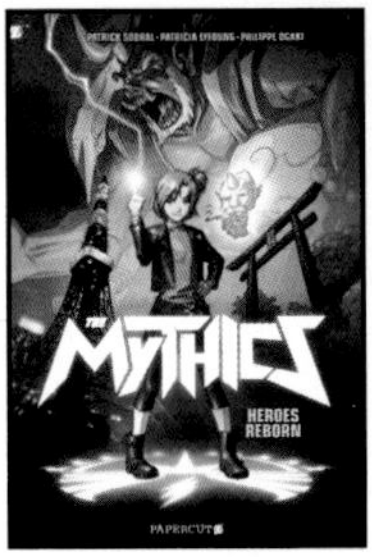
THE MYTHICS

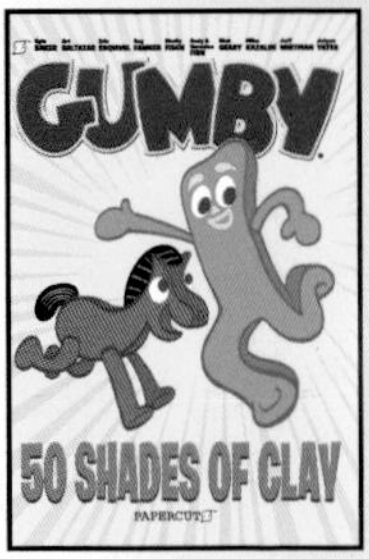
GUMBY

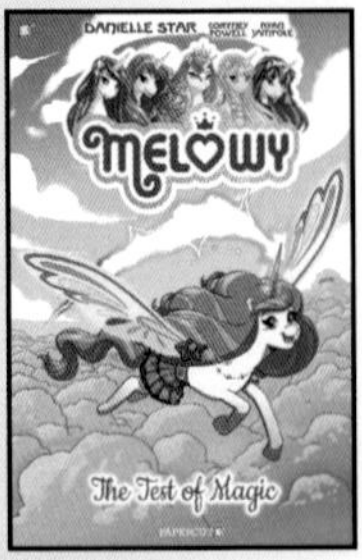
MELOWY

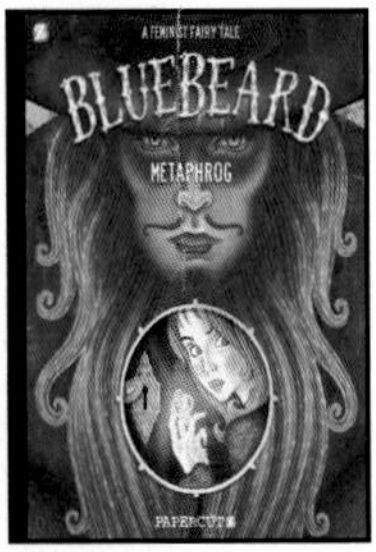
BLUEBEARD

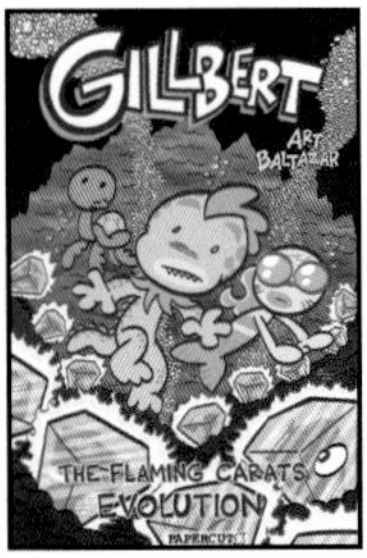
GILLBERT

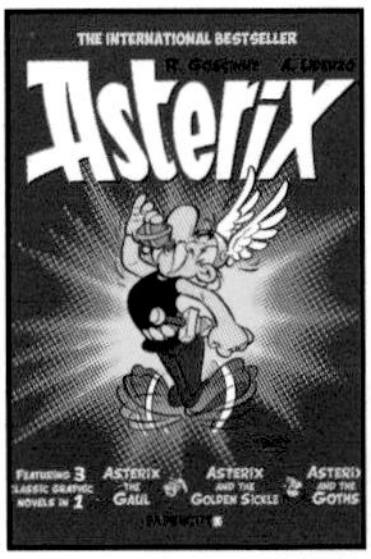
ASTERIX

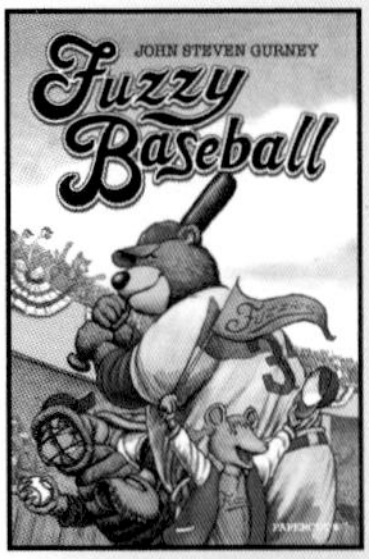
FUZZY BASEBALL

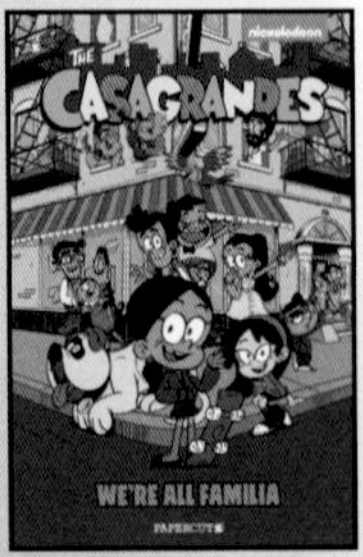
THE CASAGRANDES

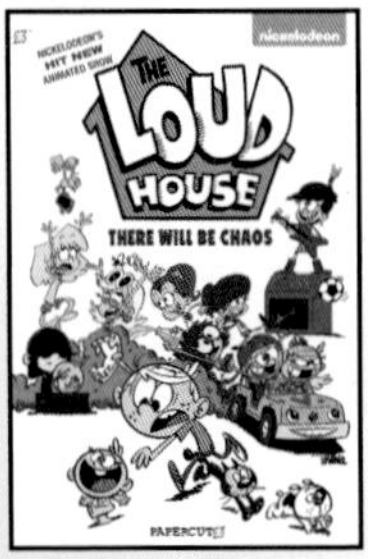
THE LOUD HOUSE

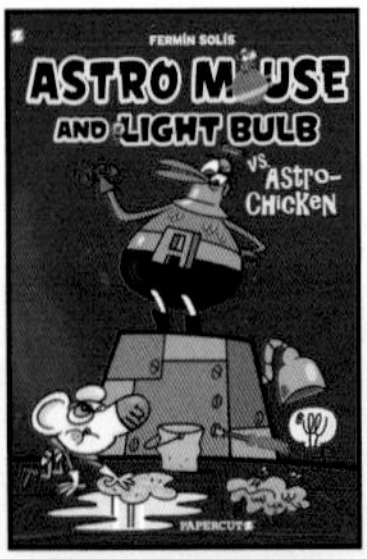
ASTRO MOUSE AND LIGHT BULB

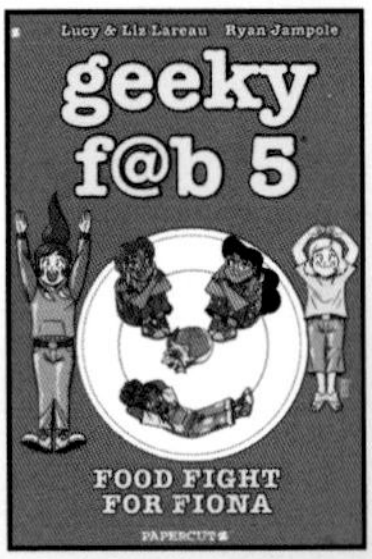
GEEKY F@B 5

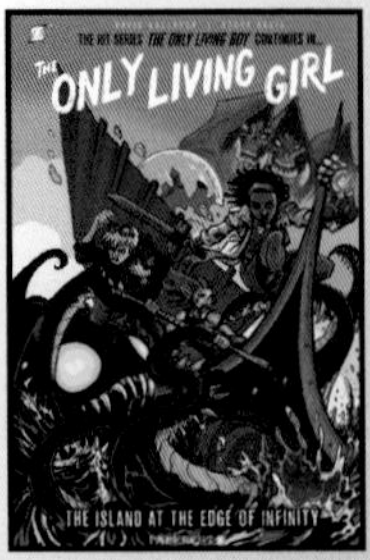
THE ONLY LIVING GIRL

papercutz.com

Also available where ebooks are sold.

THE LOUD HOUSE

BACK TO SCHOOL SPECIAL

nickelodeon™ THE LOUD HOUSE

"BACK TO SCHOOL SPECIAL"

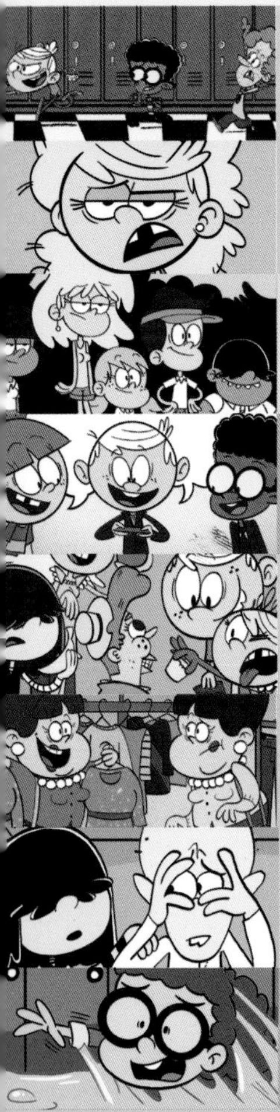

"DODGE HALL!"
Derek Fridolfs — Writer
Melissa Kleynowski — Artist
Lex Hobson — Colorist
Wilson Ramos Jr. — Letterer

"EXCHANGE OF PACE!"
Derek Fridolfs— Writer
Amanda Tran — Artist, Colorist
Wilson Ramos Jr. — Letterer

"BAD HAIR DAY!"
Erik Steinman — Writer
Joel Zamudio — Artist, Colorist
Wilson Ramos Jr. — Letterer

"TRAILER PORK"
Derek Fridolfs — Writer
Erin Hyde — Artist, Colorist
Wilson Ramos Jr. — Letterer

"WAITING…"
Jair Holguin — Writer
Amanda Lioi — Artist
Erin Rodriguez — Colorist
Wilson Ramos Jr. — Letterer

"STUDENT STORE LORE"
Amanda Fein — Writer
Lex Hobson — Artist, Colorist
Wilson Ramos Jr. — Letterer

"THE MAN WITH A MEAL PLAN"
Derek Fridolfs — Writer
Daniela Rodriguez — Artist
Lex Hobson — Colorist
Wilson Ramos Jr. — Letterer

"A FRUITLESS ENDEAVOR"
Derek Fridolfs — Writer
D.K. Terrell — Artist, Colorist
Wilson Ramos Jr. — Letterer

"HOW YOU LIKE THEM APPLES?"
Derek Fridolfs — Writer
Izzy Boyce Blanchard — Artist
Erin Rodriguez — Colorist
Wilson Ramos Jr. — Letterer

"SLEEPLESS IN PRESCHOOL"
Kara Fein — Writer
Amanda Lioi— Artist, Colorist
Wilson Ramos Jr. — Letterer

"IT SUITS YOU"
Kara and Amanda Fein — Writers
Izzy Boyce Blanchard — Artist
Lex Hobson — Colorist
Wilson Ramos Jr. — Letterer

"ALICE FORGIVEN"
Derek Fridolfs — Writer
Izzy Boyce Blanchard — Artist
Erin Rodriguez — Colorist
Wilson Ramos Jr. — Letterer

"PARADE OF FOOLS"
Kiernan Sjursen-Lien — Writer, Artist
Erin Rodriguez — Colorist
Wilson Ramos Jr. — Letterer

"INTERSTELLA"
Derek Fridolfs — Writer
Amanda Lioi — Artist, Colorist
Wilson Ramos Jr. — Letterer

"PASS CLASS OR DASH"
Rebecca E. Banks — Writer
Jennifer Hernandez — Artist, Colorist
Wilson Ramos Jr. — Letterer

"THE TEACHERS LOUNGE"
Kara and Amanda Fein — Writers
Lex Hobson — Artist, Colorist
Wilson Ramos Jr. — Letterer

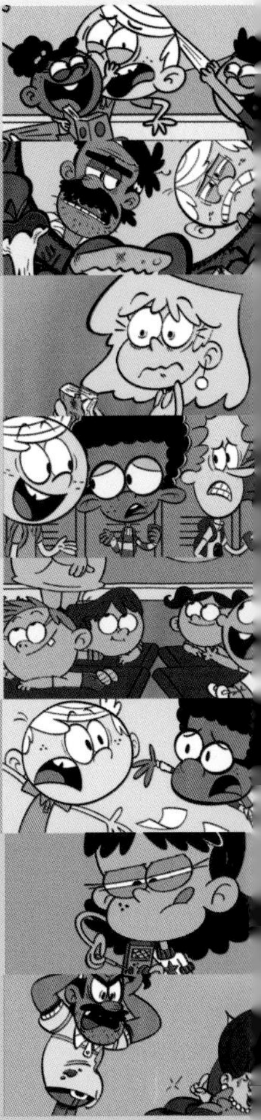

KIERNAN SJURSEN-LIEN — Cover Artist
JAYJAY JACKSON — Design
KARA FEIN, CAITLIN FEIN, KRISTEN G. SMITH, DANA CLUVERIUS, MOLLIE FREILICH, NEIL WADE, MIGUEL PUGA, LALO ALCARAZ, JOAN HILTY, KRISTEN YU-UM, EMILIE CRUZ, and ARTHUR "DJ" DESIN— Special Thanks
KARLO ANTUNES — Editor
STEPHANIE BROOKS — Assistant Managing Editor
JEFF WHITMAN — Comics Editor/Nickelodeon
MICOL HIATT — Comics Designer/Nickelodeon
JIM SALICRUP
Editor-in-Chief

ISBN: 978-1-5458-0891-7 paperback edition
ISBN: 978-1-5458-0890-0 hardcover edition

www.papercutz.com

Papercutz books may be purchased for business or promotional use. For information on bulk purchases please contact Macmillan Corporate and Premium Sales Department at (800) 221-7945 x5442.

Printed in India
June 2022

Distributed by Macmillan
First Printing

MEET THE LOUD FAMILY
and friends!

LINCOLN LOUD
THE MIDDLE CHILD

Lincoln is the middle child, with five older sisters and five younger sisters. He has learned that surviving the Loud household means staying a step ahead. He's the man with a plan, always coming up with a way to get what he wants or deal with a problem, even if things inevitably go wrong. Being the only boy comes with some perks. Lincoln gets his own room – even if it's just a converted linen closet. On the other hand, being the only boy also means he sometimes gets a little too much attention from his sisters. They mother him, tease him, and use him as the occasional lab rat or fashion show participant. Lincoln's sisters may drive him crazy, but he loves them and is always willing to help out if they need him.

LORI LOUD
THE OLDEST

As the first-born child of the Loud Clan, Lori sees herself as the boss of all her siblings. She feels she's paved the way for them and deserves extra respect. Her signature traits are rolling her eyes, texting her boyfriend, Bobby, and literally saying "literally" all the time. Because she's the oldest and most experienced sibling, Lori can be a great ally, so it pays to stay on her good side, especially since she can drive.

LENI LOUD
THE FASHIONISTA

Leni spends most of her time designing outfits and accessorizing. She always falls for Luan's pranks, and sometimes walks into walls when she's talking (she's not great at doing two things at once). Leni might be flighty, but she's the sweetest of the Loud siblings and truly has a heart of gold (even though she's pretty sure it's a heart of blood).

LUNA LOUD
THE ROCK STAR

Luna is loud, boisterous, freewheeling, and her energy is always cranked to 11. She thinks about music so much that she even talks in song lyrics. On the off-chance she doesn't have her guitar with her, everything can and will be turned into a musical instrument. You can always count on Luna to help out, and she'll do most anything you ask, as long as you're okay with her supplying a rocking guitar accompaniment.

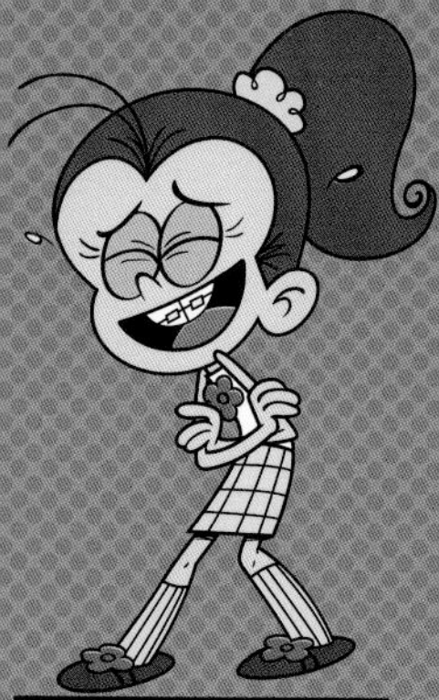

LUAN LOUD
THE JOKESTER

Luan's a standup comedienne who provides a non-stop barrage of silly puns. She's big on prop comedy too – squirting flowers and whoopee cushions – so you have to be on your toes whenever she's around. She loves to pull pranks and is a really good ventriloquist – she is often found doing bits with her dummy, Mr. Coconuts. Luan never lets anything get her down; to her, laughter IS the best medicine.

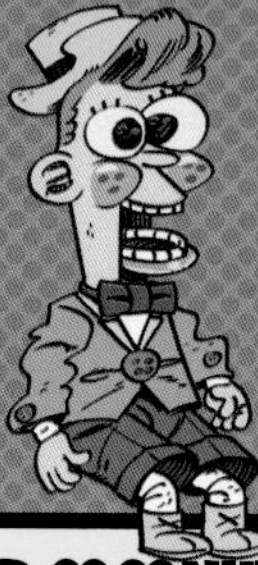

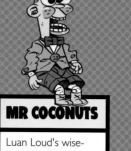

MR COCONUTS

Luan Loud's wise-cracking dummy.

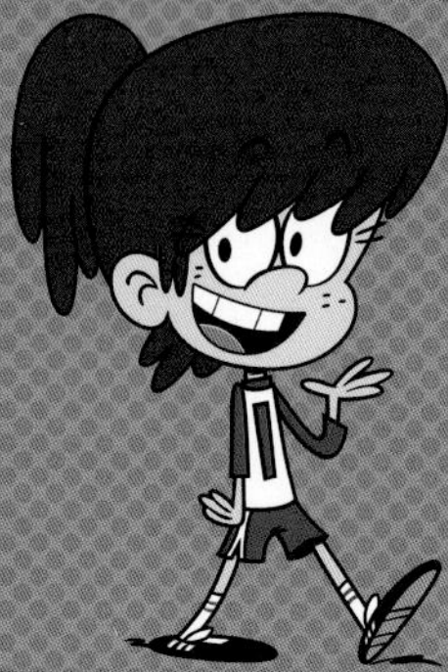

LYNN LOUD
THE ATHLETE

Lynn is athletic and full of energy and is always looking for a teammate. With her, it's all sports all the time. She'll turn any-thing into a sport. Putting away eggs? Jump shot! Score! Cleaning up the eggs? Slap shot! Score! Lynn is very competitive, but despite her competitive nature, she always tries to just have a good time.

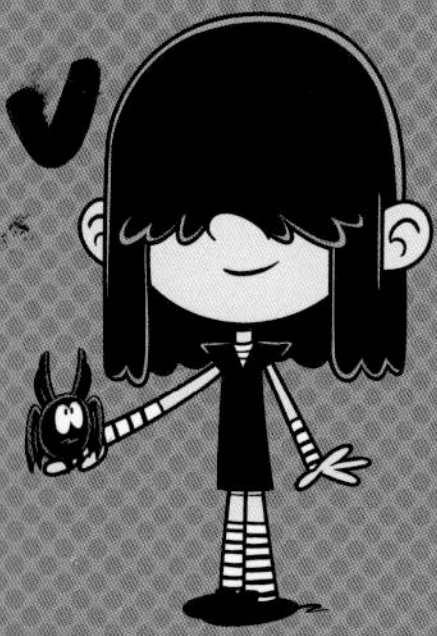

LUCY LOUD
THE EMO

You can always count on Lucy to give the morbid point of view in any given situation. She is obsessed with all things spooky and dark – funerals, vampires, séances, and the like. She wears mostly black and writes moody poetry. She's usually quiet and keeps to herself. Lucy has a way of mysteriously appearing out of nowhere, and try as they might, her siblings never get used to this.

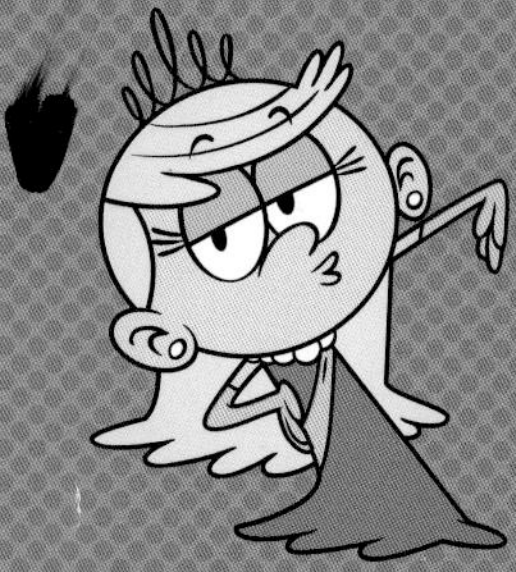

LOLA LOUD
THE BEAUTY QUEEN)

Lola could not be more different from her twin sister, Lana. She's a pageant powerhouse whose interests include glitter, photo shoots, and her own beautiful, beautiful face. But don't let her cute, gap-toothed smile fool you; underneath all the sugar and spice lurks a Machiavellian mastermind. Whatever Lola wants, Lola gets – or else. She's the eyes and ears of the household and never resists an opportunity to tattle on troublemakers. But if you stay on Lola's good side, you've got yourself a fierce ally – and a lifetime supply of free makeovers.

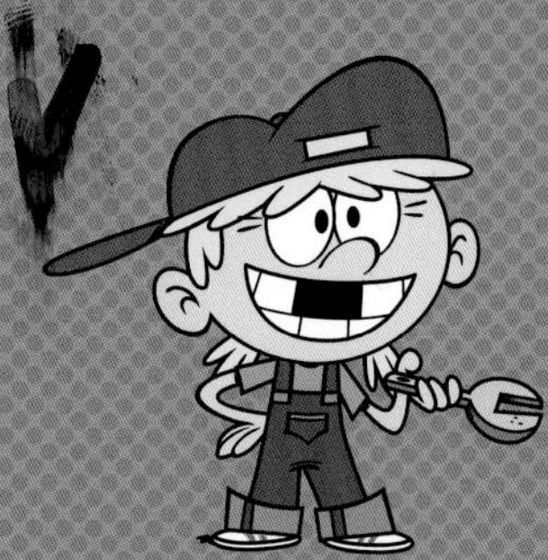

LANA LOUD
THE TOMBOY

Lana is the rough-and-tumble sparkplug counterpart to her twin sister, Lola. She's all about reptiles, mud pies, and muffler repair. She's the resident Ms. Fix-it and is always ready to lend a hand – the dirtier the job, the better. Need your toilet unclogged? Snake fed? Back-zit popped? Lana's your gal. All she asks in return is a little A-B-C gum, or a handful of kibble (she often sneaks it from the dog bowl).

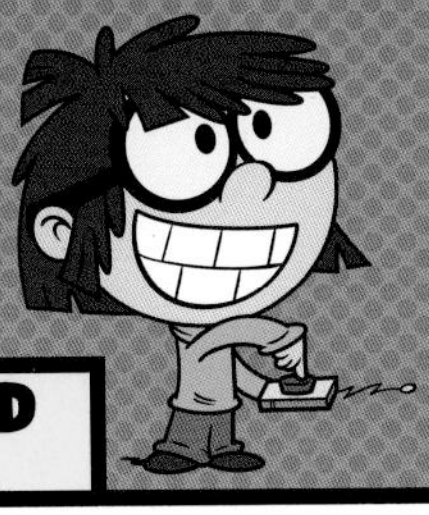

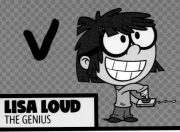

LISA LOUD
THE GENIUS

Lisa is smarter than the rest of her siblings combined. She'll most likely be a rocket scientist, or a brain surgeon, or an evil genius who takes over the world. Lisa spends most of her time working in her lab (the family has gotten used to the explosions), and says her research leaves little time for frivolous human pursuits like "playing" or "getting haircuts." That said, she's always there to help with a homework question, or to explain why the sky is blue, or to point out the structural flaws in someone's pillow fort. Lisa says it's the least she can do for her favorite test subjects, er, siblings.

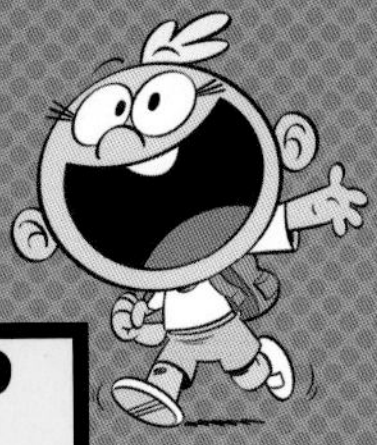

LILY LOUD
THE BABY

Lily's the baby of the family, but she's growing up fast. She's a toddler now and can speak full sentences – well, sometimes. As an infant she was already mischievous, but now she's upped her game. No matter what, though, she still brings a smile to everyone's faces, and the family loves her unconditionally.

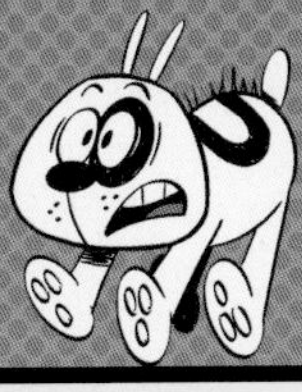

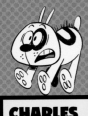

CHARLES

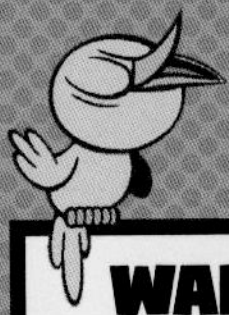

WALT

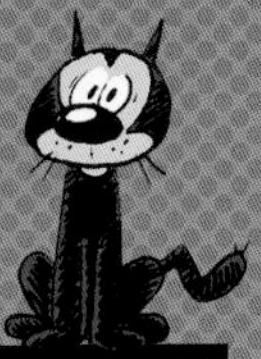

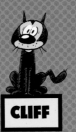

CLIFF

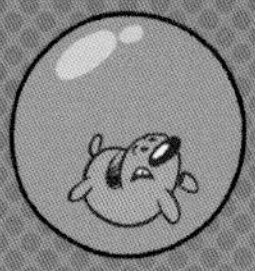

GEO

RITA LOUD

Mother to the eleven Loud kids, Mom (Rita Loud) wears many different hats. She's a chauffeur, homework-checker, and barf-cleaner-upper all rolled into one. She's always there for her kids and ready to jump into action during a crisis, whether it's a fight between the twins or Leni's missing shoe. When she's not chasing the kids around or at her day job as a dental hygienist, Mom pursues her passion: writing. She also loves taking on house projects and is very handy with tools (guess that's where Lana gets it from). Between writing, working, and being a mom, her days are always hectic but she wouldn't have it any other way.

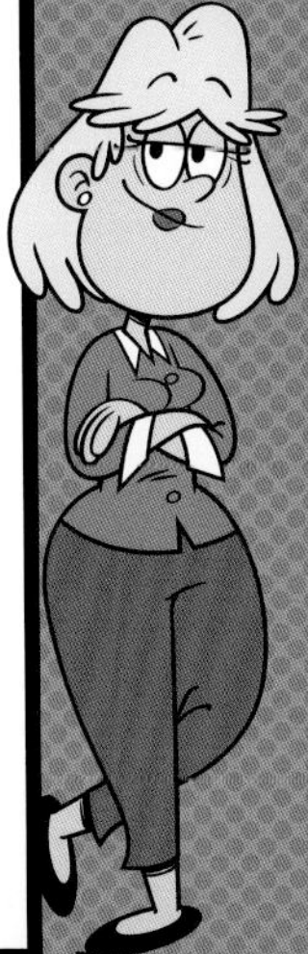

LYNN LOUD SR.

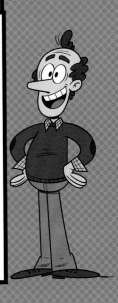

Dad (Lynn Loud Sr.) is a fun-loving, upbeat aspiring chef. A kid-at-heart, he's not above taking part in the kids' zany schemes. In addition to cooking, Dad loves his van, playing the cowbell, and making puns. Before meeting Mom, Dad spent a semester in England and has been obsessed with British culture ever since – and sometimes "accidentally" slips into a British accent. When Dad's not wrangling the kids, he's pursuing his dream of opening his own restaurant where he hopes to make his "Lynn-sagnas" world-famous.

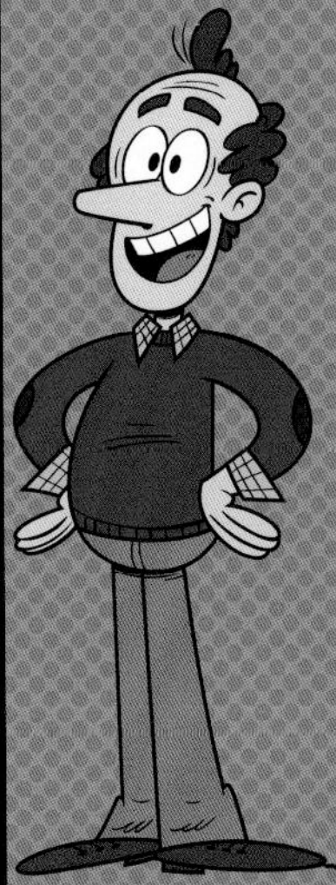

CLYDE McBRIDE
THE BEST FRIEND

Clyde is Lincoln's partner in crime. He's always willing to go along with Lincoln's crazy schemes (even if he sees the flaws in them up-front). Lincoln and Clyde are two peas in a pod and share pretty much all of the same tastes in movies, comics, TV shows, toys – you name it. As an only child, Clyde envies Lincoln – how cool would it be to always have siblings around to talk to? But since Clyde spends so much time at the Loud household, he's almost an honorary sibling anyway.

ZACH GURDLE

Zach is a self-admitted nerd who's obsessed with aliens and conspiracy theories. He lives between a freeway and a circus, so the chaos of the Loud House doesn't faze him. He and Rusty occasionally butt heads, but deep down, it's all love.

RUSTY SPOKES

Rusty is a self-proclaimed ladies' man who's always the first to dish out girl advice – even though he's never been on an actual date. His dad owns a suit rental service, so occasionally Rusty can hook the gang up with some dapper duds – just as long as no one gets anything dirty.

LIAM HUNNICUTT

Liam is an enthusiastic, sweet-natured farm boy full of down-home wisdom. He loves hanging out with his Mee Maw, wrestling his prize pig Virginia, and sharing his farm-to-table produce with the rest of the gang.

STELLA ZHAU

Stella, is a quirky, carefree girl who's new to Royal Woods. She has tons of interests, such as trying on wigs, playing laser tag, eating curly fries, and hanging with her friends. But what she loves the most is tech — she always wants to dismantle electronics and put them back together again.

RONNIE ANNE SANTIAGO

Ronnie Anne's a skateboarding city girl now. She's fearless, free-spirited, and always quick to come up with a plan. She's one tough cookie, but she also has a sweet side. Ronnie Anne loves helping her family, and that's taught her to help others, too. When she's not pitching in at the family *mercado*, you can find her exploring the neighborhood with her best friend Sid, or ordering hot dogs with her skater buds Casey, Nikki, and Sameer.

BOBBY SANTIAGO

Bobby is Ronnie Anne's big bro. He's a student and one of the hardest workers in the city! He loves his family and loves working at the *mercado*. As his *abuelo's* right hand man, Bobby can't wait to take over the family business one day. He's a big kid at heart, and his clumsiness gets him into some sticky situations at work, like locking himself in the freezer. *Mercado* mishaps aside, everyone in the neighborhood loves to come to the store and talk to Bobby.

MARIA CASAGRANDE SANTIAGO

She's the mother of Bobby and Ronnie Anne. A hardworking nurse, she doesn't get to spend a lot of time with her kids, but when she does she treasures it. Maria is calm and rational but often worries about whether she's doing enough for her kids. Maria, Bobby, and Ronnie Anne are a close-knit trio who were used to having only each other – until they moved in with their extended family.

SERGIO

Sergio is the Casagrandes' beloved pet parrot. He's a blunt, sassy bird who "thinks" he's full of wisdom and always has something to say. The Casagrandes have to keep a close eye on their credit card as Sergio is addicted to online shopping and is always asking the family to buy him some new gadget he saw on TV. Sergio is most loyal to Rosa and serves as her wing-man, partner in crime, taste tester, and confidant. He can be found trying to get his ex-girlfriend, Priscilla (an ostrich at the zoo), to respond to him.

HECTOR CASAGRANDE

Hector is Carlos and Maria's dad, and the *abuelo* of the family (that means grandpa)! He owns the *mercado* on the ground floor of their apartment building and takes great pride in his work, his family, and being the unofficial "mayor" of the block. He loves to tell stories, share his ideas, and gossip (even though he won't admit to it). You can find him working in the *mercado*, playing guitar, or watching his favorite *telenovela*.

ROSA CASAGRANDE

Rosa is Carlos and Maria's mom and the *abuela* of the family (that means grandma)! She's the head of the household, the wisest Casagrande, and the master cook with a superhuman ability to tell when anyone in the house is hungry. She often tries to fix problems or illnesses with traditional Mexican home remedies and potions. She's very protective of her family... sometimes a little too much.

CARLOS CASAGRANDE

Carlos is Maria's brother. He's married to Frida, and together they have four kids: Carlota, C.J., Carl, and Carlitos. Carlos is a Professor of Cultural Studies at a local college. Usually he has his head in the clouds or his nose in a textbook. Relatively easygoing, Carlos is a loving father and an enthusiastic teacher who tries to get his kids interested in their Mexican heritage.

FRIDA PUGA CASAGRANDE

Frida is Carlos, C.J., Carl, and Carlitos' mom. She's an art professor and a performance artist, and is always looking for new ways to express herself. She's got a big heart and isn't shy about her emotions. Frida tends to cry when she's sad, happy, angry, or any other emotion you can think of. She's always up for fun, is passionate about her art, and loves her family more than anything.

CARLOTA CASAGRANDE

Carlota is CJ, Carl, and Carlitos' older sister. A social media influencer, she's excited to be like a big sister to Ronnie Anne. She's a force to be reckoned with, and is always trying to share her distinctive vintage style tips with Ronnie Anne.

CJ (CARLOS JR.) CASAGRANDE

CJ is Carlota's younger brother and Carl and Carlitos' older brother. He was born with Down Syndrome. He lights up any room with his infectious smile and is always ready to play. He's obsessed with pirates and is BFFs with Bobby. He likes to wear a bowtie to any family occasion, and you can always catch him laughing or helping his *abuela*.

CARL CASAGRANDE

Carl is wise beyond his years. He's confident, outgoing, and puts a lot of time and effort into looking good. He likes to think of himself as a suave businessman and doesn't like to get caught playing with his action figures or wearing his footie PJs. Even though Bobby is nothing but nice to him, Carl sees his big cousin as his biggest rival.

CARLITOS CASAGRANDE

Carlitos is the baby of the family, and is always copying the behavior of everyone in the household – even if they aren't human. He's a playful and silly baby who loves to play with the family pets.

LALO

Lalo is a slobbery bull mastiff who thinks he's a lapdog. He's not the smartest pup and gets scared easily… but he loves his family and loves to cuddle.

HAIKU	MORPHEUS	PERSEPHONE	DANTE	BERTRAND	BORIS

MORTICIANS CLUB

MS. GALIANO

Ms. Galiano is Ronnie Anne and the skater kids' teacher at Cesar Chavez Academy. She is sweet as pie and often relies on the kids to keep her up to date on the new, hip, pop culture trends. She briefly dated Ronnie Anne's dad, Arturo, and even though it didn't work out, they still remain friends.

COACH CRAWFORD

Coach Crawford is Cesar Chavez Academy's gruff PE teacher. Militant in his approach and a traditionalist as far as what he considers a "sport," Coach Crawford is willing to adjust his stance on things if it means he can just drink his coffee in peace. Now in retirement, Coach Crawford stays active by occasionally subbing in for new PE teacher, Mrs. Kernicky, much to the dismay of the students.

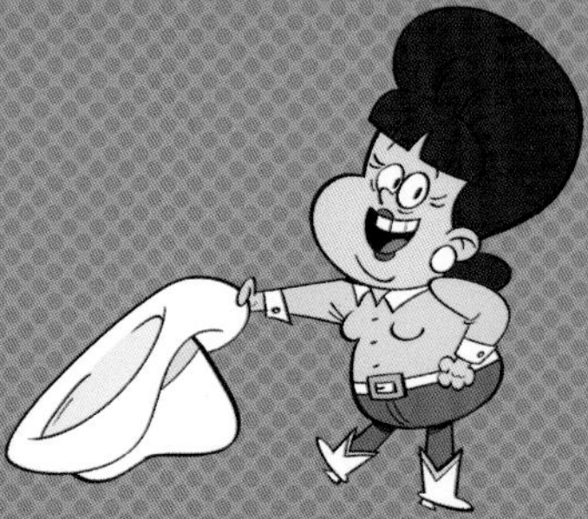

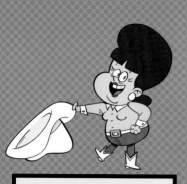

CHERYL FARRELL

Cheryl is the secretary at Royal Woods Elementary School and identical twin to Meryl, who lovingly calls her "Cher-Bear!" She is a bubbly Southerner who is always rooting for the students at Royal Woods Elementary. She loves boot scootin', storing items in her signature beehive hairdo, and watching soap operas with her sister in their shared condo.

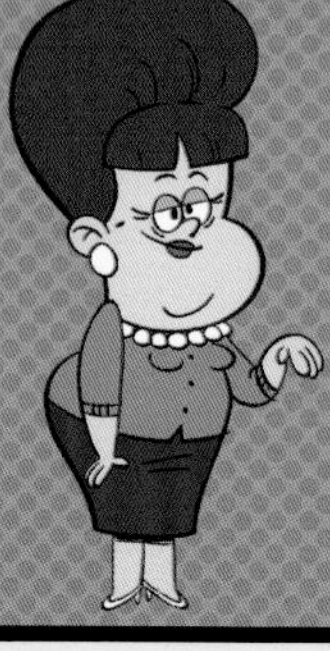

MERYL FARRELL

Meryl is the secretary at Royal Woods Middle School and identical twin to Cheryl. Like her sister, she is a charming Southerner and loves gossip, karaoke, and soap operas. She has a sweet way of talking (comparing things to baked goods) and is always eager to help students when they need her.

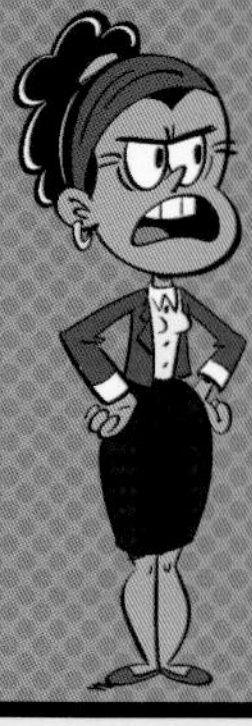

PRINCIPAL RAMIREZ

Principal Ramirez runs Royal Woods Middle School. She is firm when she needs to be but also super enthusiastic with the students, always there to cheer them on. She's got a soft spot for the school's Action News Team, no matter how many times their shenanigans make her life difficult. And she's always open to creative problem solving, even if it means temporarily sending Lincoln to a school in Canada!

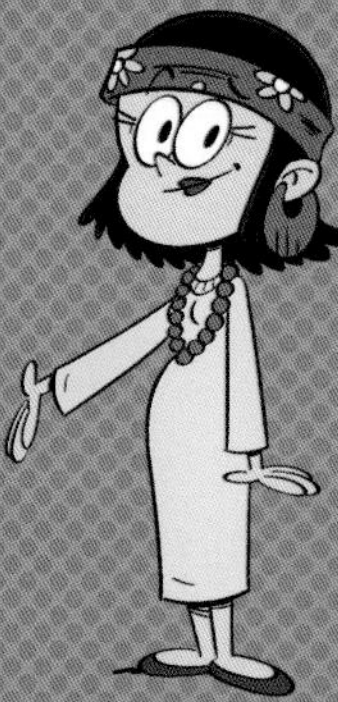

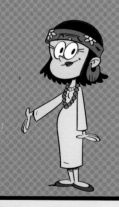

MRS. SALTER

Mrs. Salter is the most popular teacher at Royal Woods Middle School due to her classroom juice bar. Mrs. Salter is a free spirit who has a passion for making education fun! Rusty, Liam, Clyde, Zach, and Stella are lucky enough to be her students while Lincoln has to watch the fun from afar in Mr. Bolhofner's class...

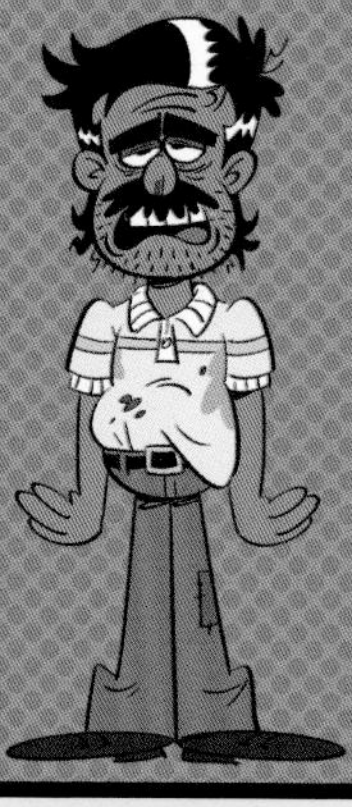

MR. BOLHOFNER

Mr. Bolhofner is Lincoln's gruff but well-meaning middle school teacher, whose stories of survival out in the wild are renowned throughout Royal Woods. He has a passion for smoked jerky and taxidermy, and a flair for playing the bass drum. He has two fierce pets that usually cause trouble at school: a piranha named Hank and a bobcat named Rocket. Although school rumors suggest that Bolhofner is scary enough to warrant the nickname "Skullhofner," Lincoln and his friends know that there's a big softie underneath his hard exterior.

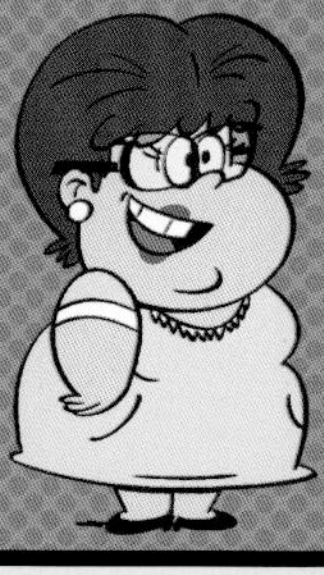

DR. SHUTTLEWORTH

Dr. Shuttleworth runs the prestigious Baby Bunker Preschool, where Lily is a student. She is a kind, sophisticated educator who expresses pride in her students and encourages creativity and good manners. If you want to be in her class, you better be potty-trained!

"DODGE HALL!"

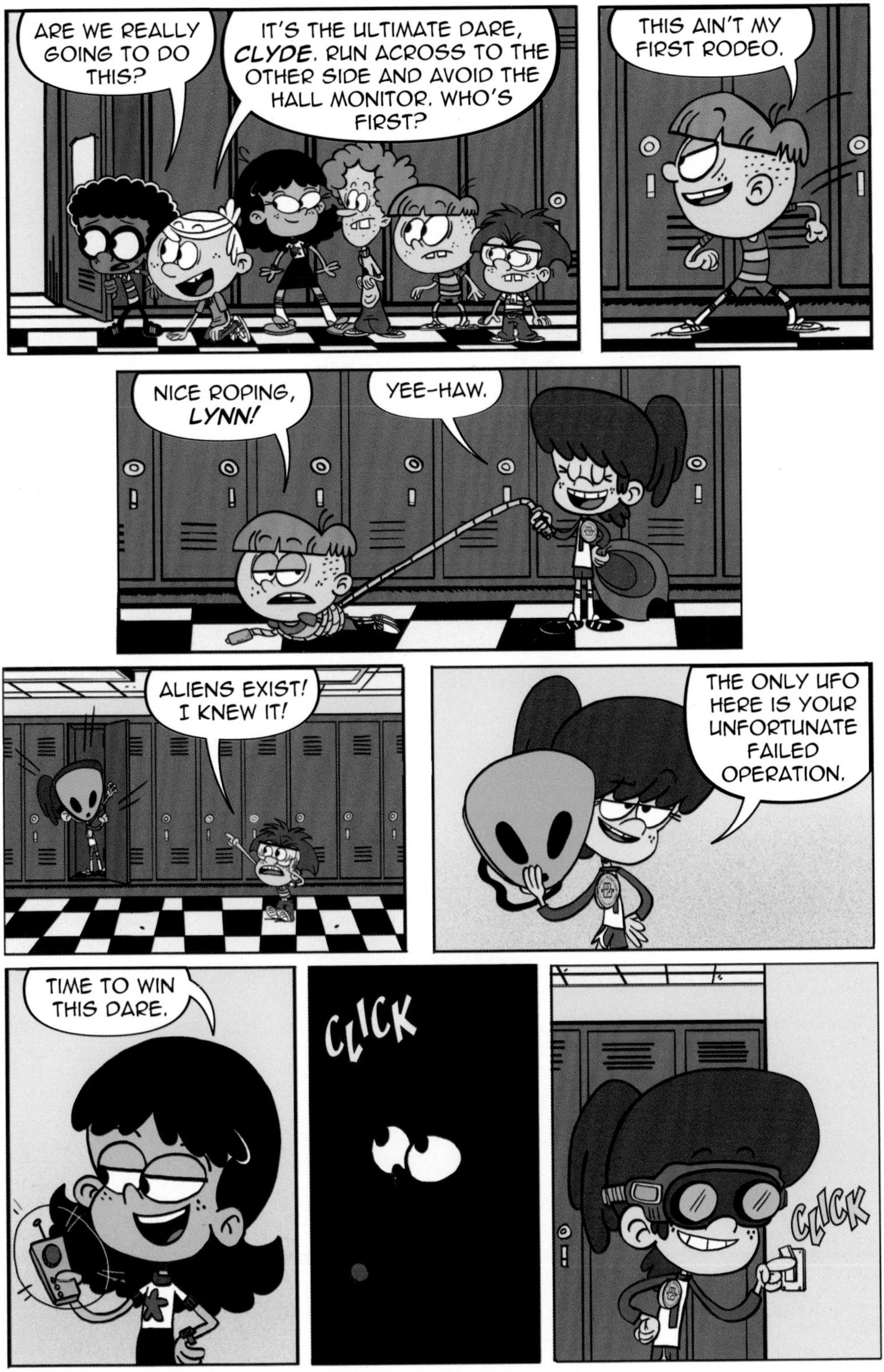

ARE WE REALLY GOING TO DO THIS?
IT'S THE ULTIMATE DARE, CLYDE. RUN ACROSS TO THE OTHER SIDE AND AVOID THE HALL MONITOR. WHO'S FIRST?
THIS AIN'T MY FIRST RODEO.
NICE ROPING, LYNN!
YEE-HAW.
ALIENS EXIST! I KNEW IT!
THE ONLY UFO HERE IS YOUR UNFORTUNATE FAILED OPERATION.
TIME TO WIN THIS DARE.
CLICK
CLICK

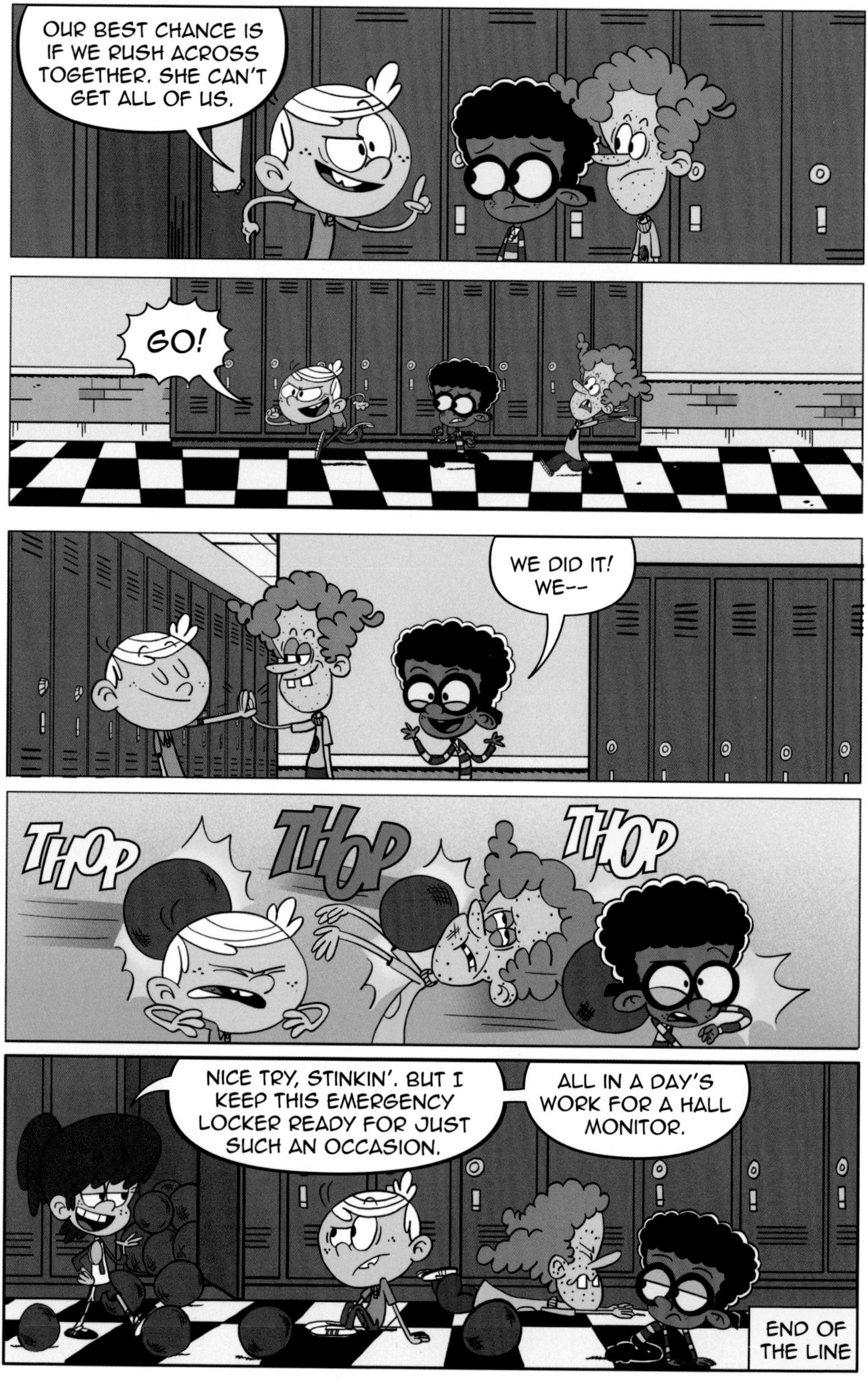
OUR BEST CHANCE IS IF WE RUSH ACROSS TOGETHER. SHE CAN'T GET ALL OF US.
GO!
WE DID IT! WE--
THOP
THOP
THOP
NICE TRY, STINKIN'. BUT I KEEP THIS EMERGENCY LOCKER READY FOR JUST SUCH AN OCCASION.
ALL IN A DAY'S WORK FOR A HALL MONITOR.
END OF THE LINE

"BAD HAIR DAY!"

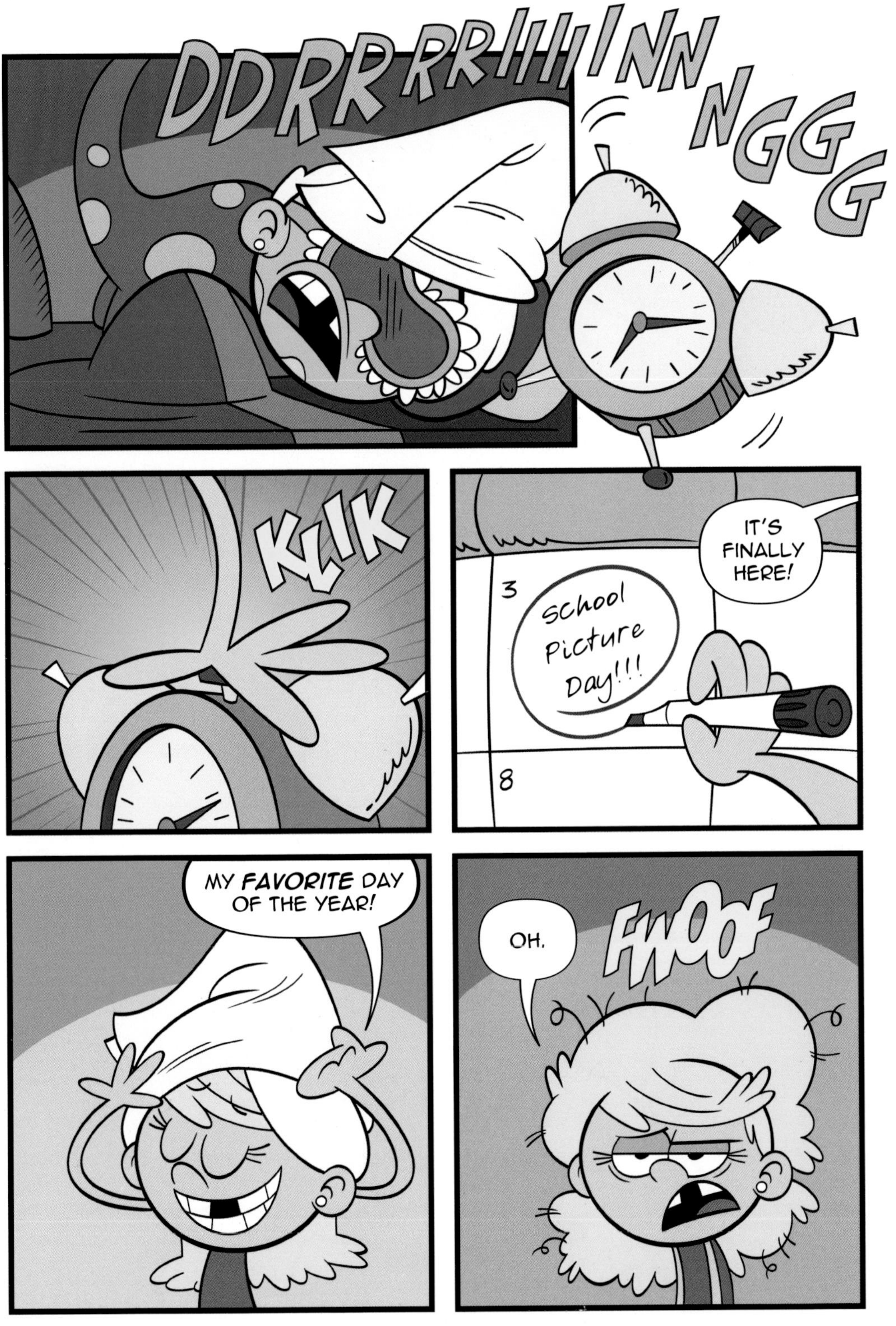
DDRRRRIIIIINNNGGG
KLIK
IT'S FINALLY HERE!
3
School Picture Day!!!
8
MY FAVORITE DAY OF THE YEAR!
OH.
FWOOF

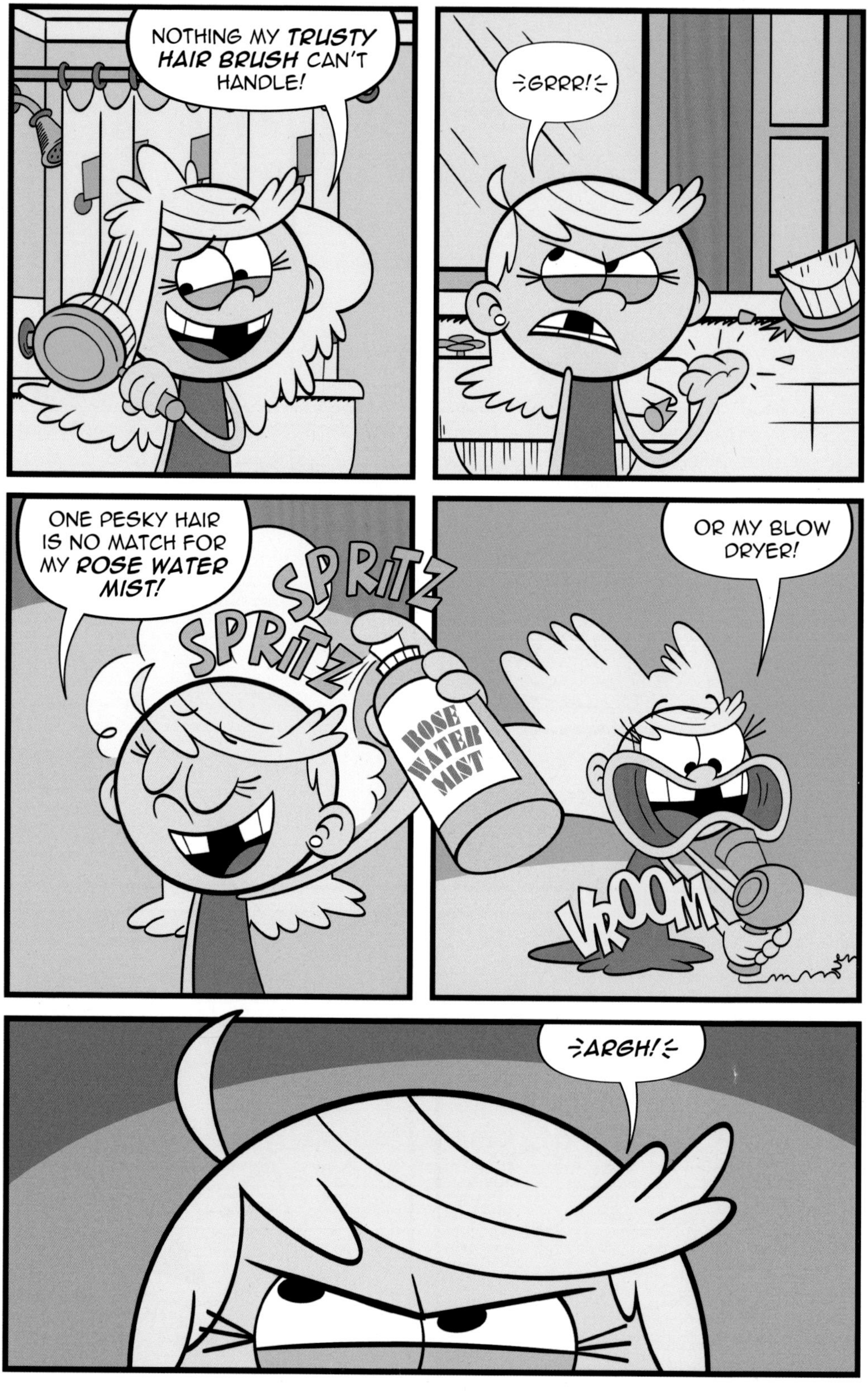
NOTHING MY **TRUSTY HAIR BRUSH** CAN'T HANDLE!
GRRR!
ONE PESKY HAIR IS NO MATCH FOR MY **ROSE WATER MIST!**
SPRITZ
SPRITZ
ROSE WATER MIST
OR MY BLOW DRYER!
VROOM
ARGH!

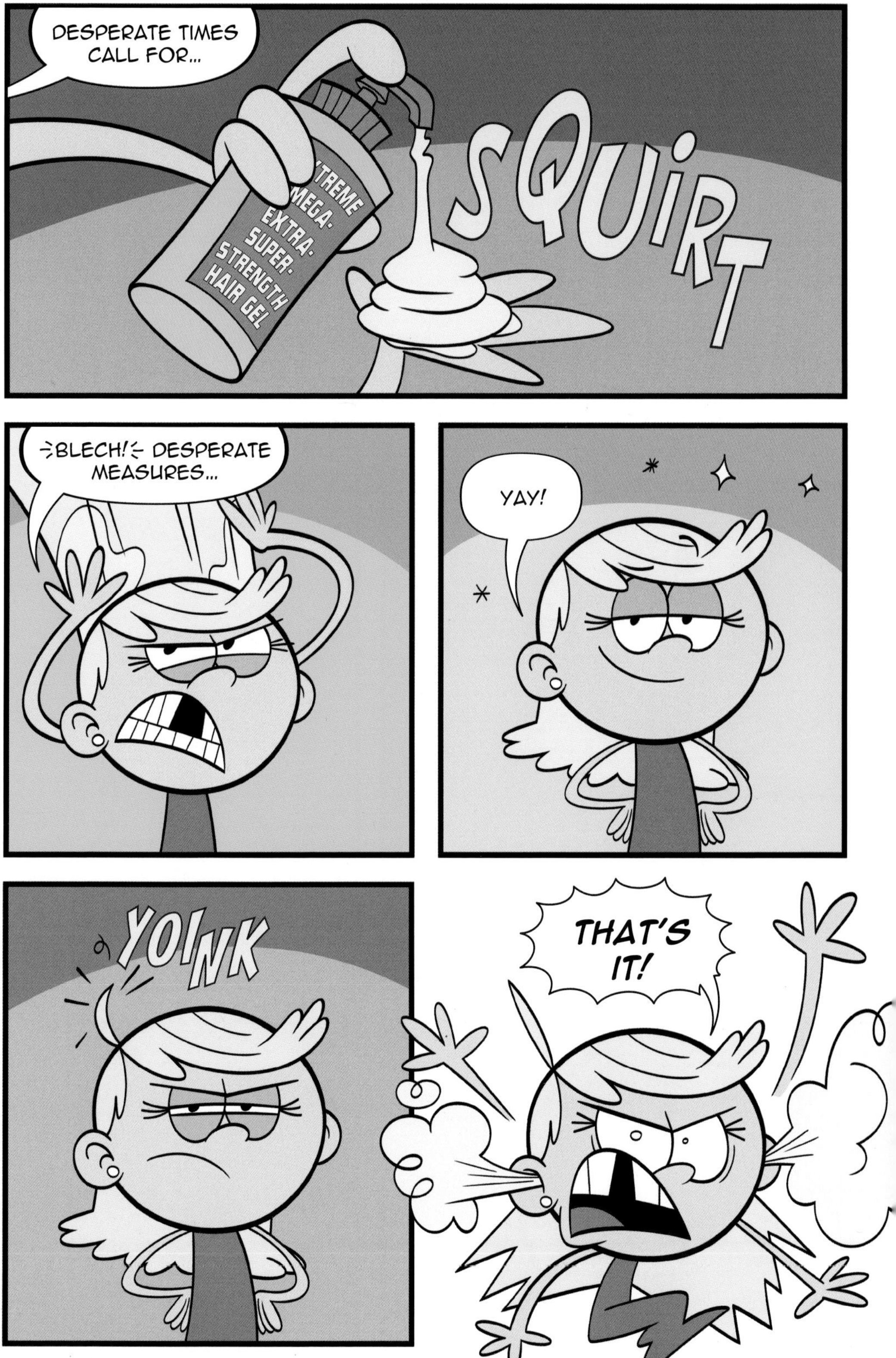
DESPERATE TIMES CALL FOR...
'TREME MEGA-EXTRA-SUPER-STRENGTH HAIR GEL
SQUIRT
BLECH! DESPERATE MEASURES...
YAY!
YOINK
THAT'S IT!

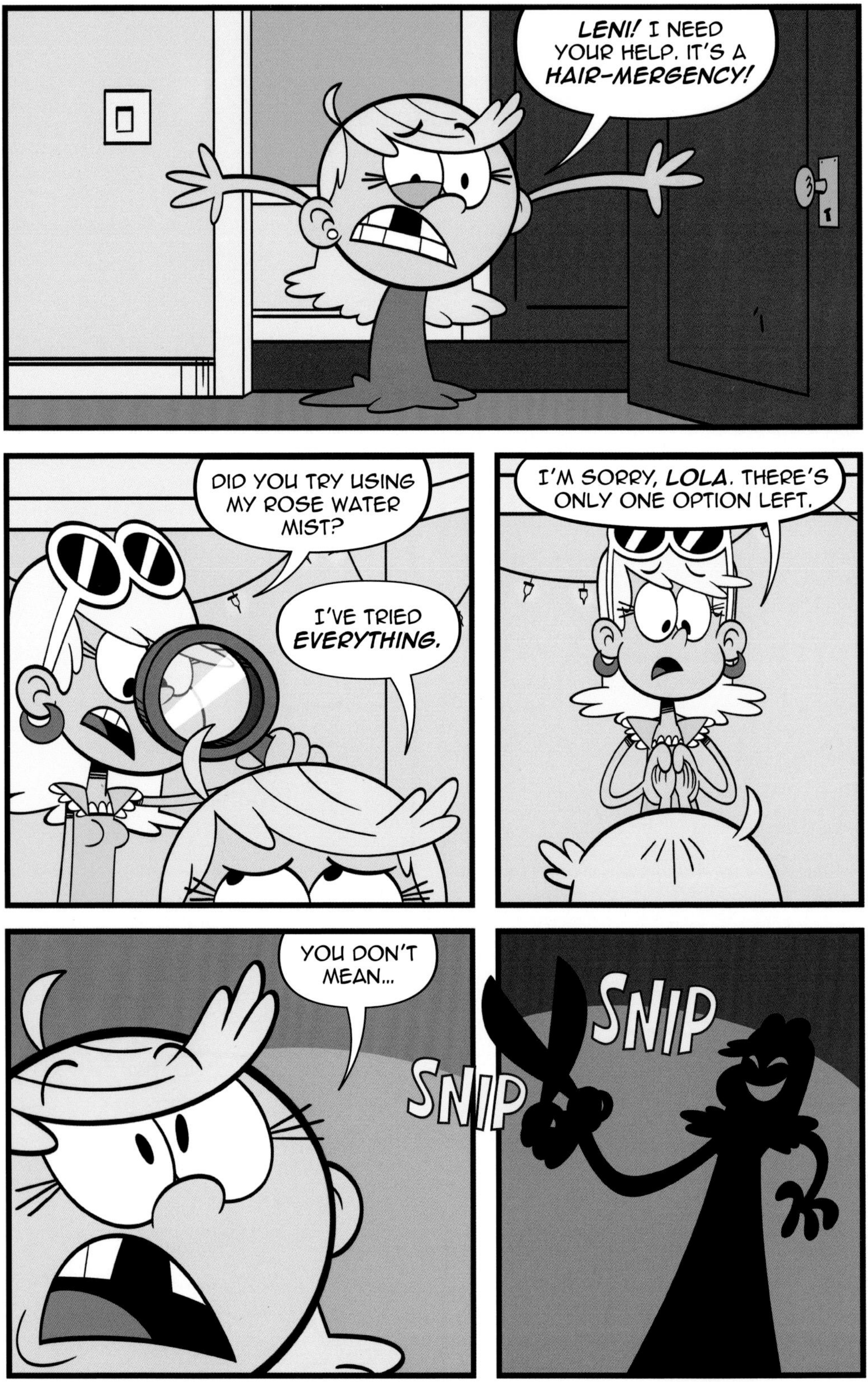
LENI! I NEED YOUR HELP. IT'S A HAIR-MERGENCY!
DID YOU TRY USING MY ROSE WATER MIST?
I'VE TRIED EVERYTHING.
I'M SORRY, LOLA. THERE'S ONLY ONE OPTION LEFT.
YOU DON'T MEAN...
SNIP
SNIP

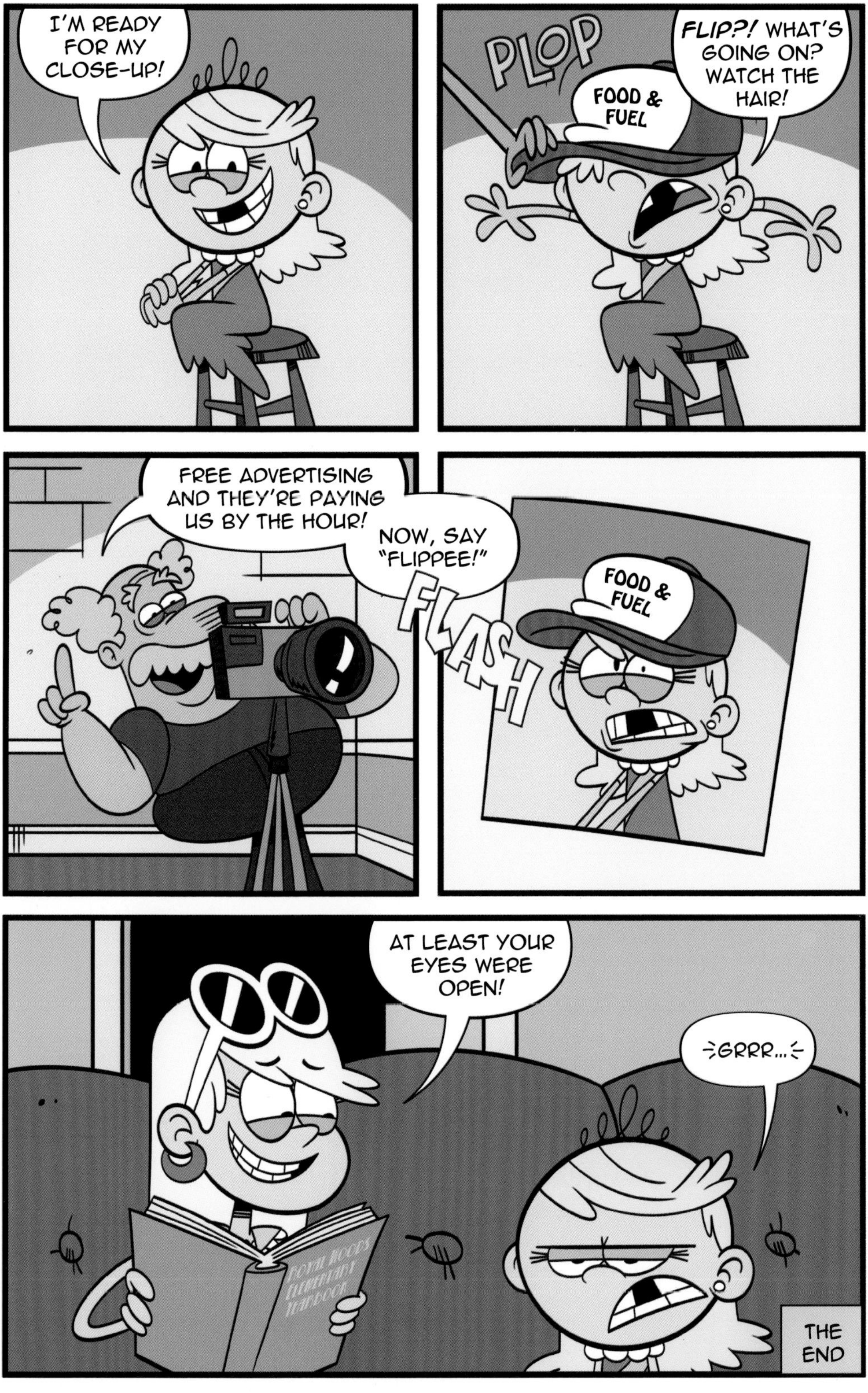

I'M READY FOR MY CLOSE-UP!
PLOP
FOOD & FUEL
FLIP?! WHAT'S GOING ON? WATCH THE HAIR!
FREE ADVERTISING AND THEY'RE PAYING US BY THE HOUR!
NOW, SAY "FLIPPEE!"
FLASH
FOOD & FUEL
AT LEAST YOUR EYES WERE OPEN!
GRRR...
THE END

"WAITING..."

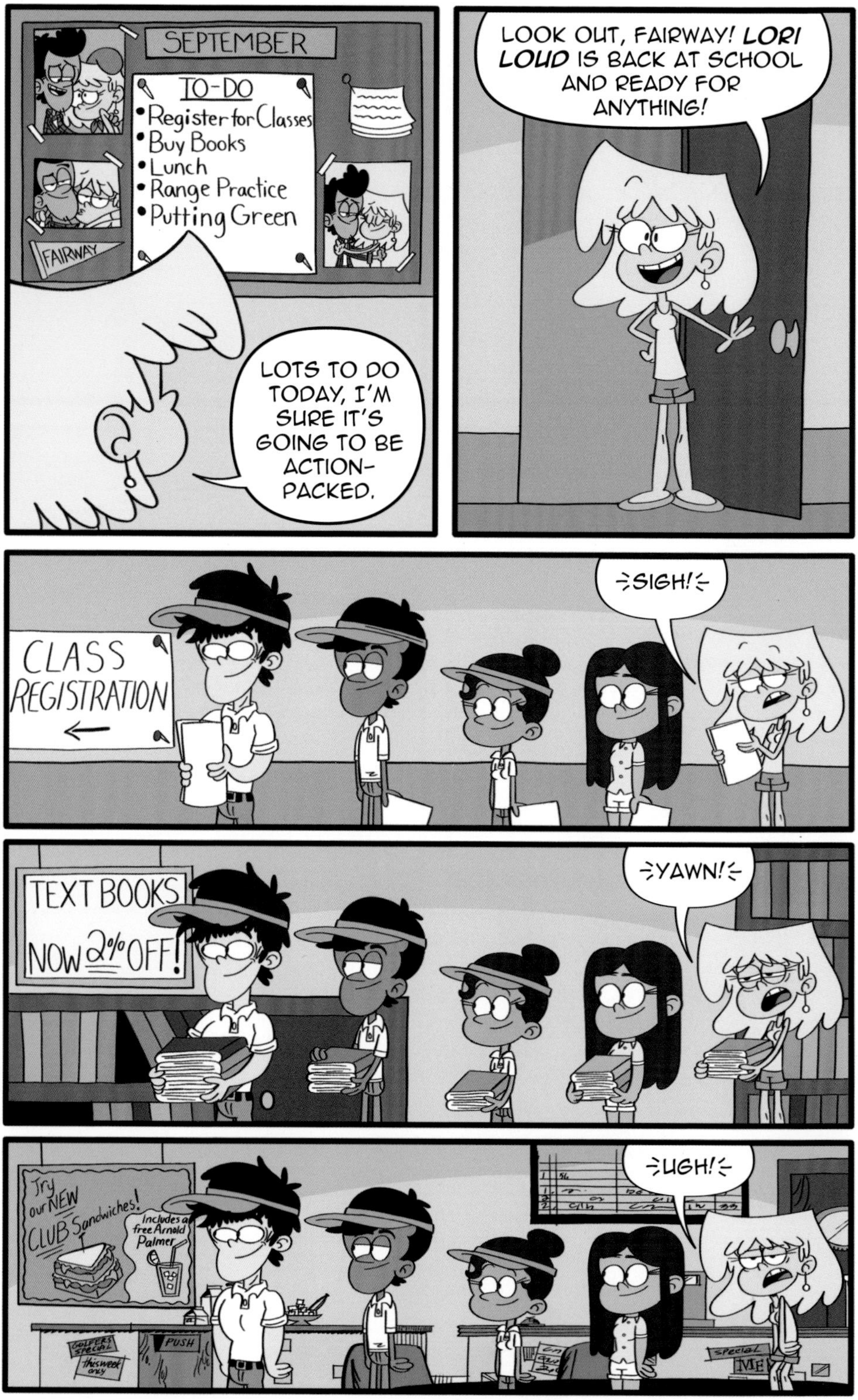
SEPTEMBER
TO-DO
• Register for Classes
• Buy Books
• Lunch
• Range Practice
• Putting Green
FAIRWAY
LOTS TO DO TODAY, I'M SURE IT'S GOING TO BE ACTION-PACKED.
LOOK OUT, FAIRWAY! LORI LOUD IS BACK AT SCHOOL AND READY FOR ANYTHING!
CLASS REGISTRATION
SIGH!
TEXT BOOKS NOW 2% OFF!
YAWN!
Try our NEW CLUB Sandwiches!
Includes a free Arnold Palmer
PUSH
UGH!

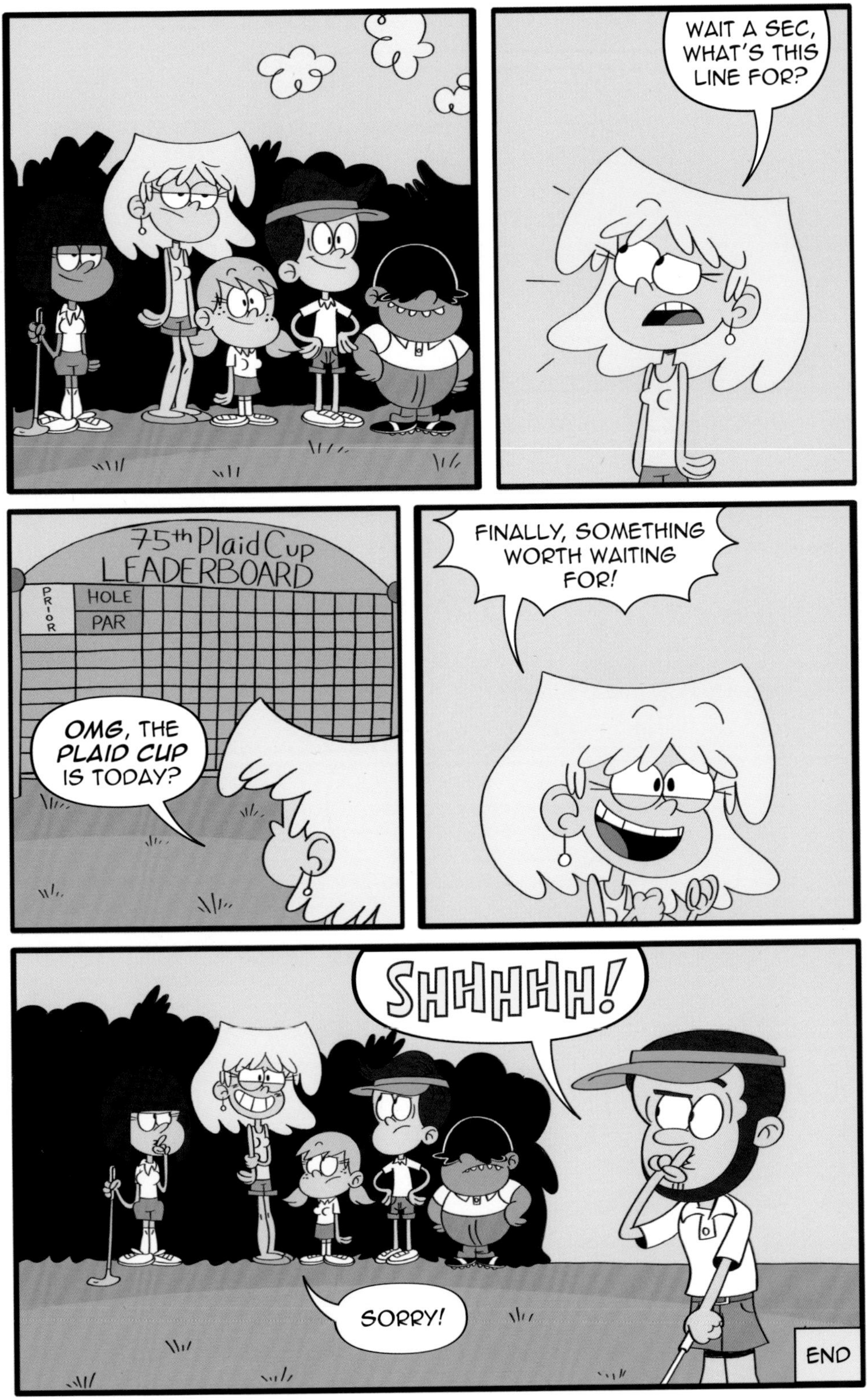
WAIT A SEC, WHAT'S THIS LINE FOR?
75th Plaid Cup LEADERBOARD
PRIOR
HOLE
PAR
OMG, THE PLAID CUP IS TODAY?
FINALLY, SOMETHING WORTH WAITING FOR!
SHHHHH!
SORRY!
END

"THE MAN WITH A MEAL PLAN"

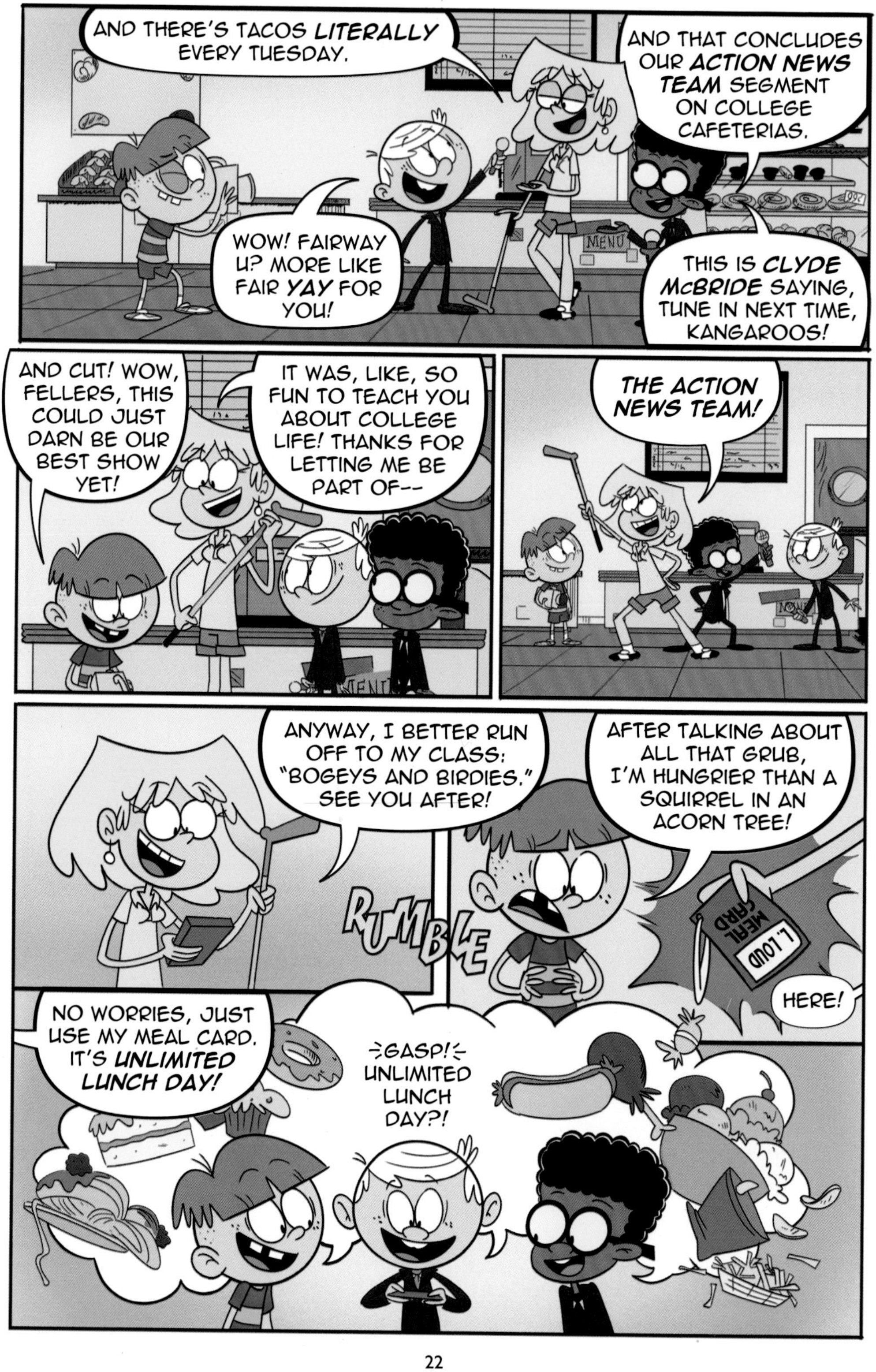
AND THERE'S TACOS LITERALLY EVERY TUESDAY.
AND THAT CONCLUDES OUR ACTION NEWS TEAM SEGMENT ON COLLEGE CAFETERIAS.
WOW! FAIRWAY U? MORE LIKE FAIR YAY FOR YOU!
MENU
THIS IS CLYDE McBRIDE SAYING, TUNE IN NEXT TIME, KANGAROOS!
AND CUT! WOW, FELLERS, THIS COULD JUST DARN BE OUR BEST SHOW YET!
IT WAS, LIKE, SO FUN TO TEACH YOU ABOUT COLLEGE LIFE! THANKS FOR LETTING ME BE PART OF--
THE ACTION NEWS TEAM!
ANYWAY, I BETTER RUN OFF TO MY CLASS: "BOGEYS AND BIRDIES." SEE YOU AFTER!
RUMBLE
AFTER TALKING ABOUT ALL THAT GRUB, I'M HUNGRIER THAN A SQUIRREL IN AN ACORN TREE!
L.LOUD MEAL CARD
HERE!
NO WORRIES, JUST USE MY MEAL CARD. IT'S UNLIMITED LUNCH DAY!
GASP! UNLIMITED LUNCH DAY?!

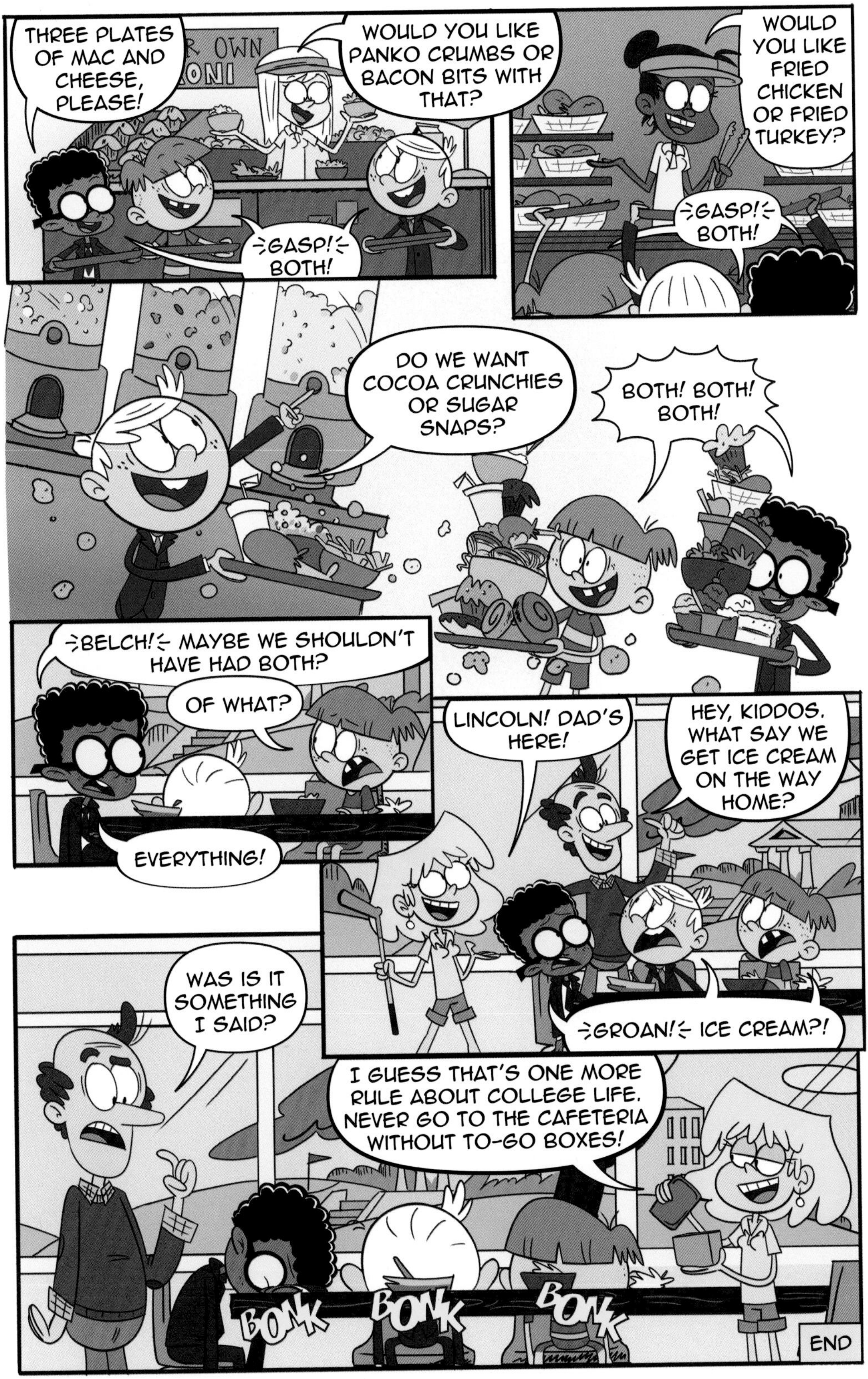
THREE PLATES OF MAC AND CHEESE, PLEASE!
WOULD YOU LIKE PANKO CRUMBS OR BACON BITS WITH THAT?
⁼GASP!⁼ BOTH!
WOULD YOU LIKE FRIED CHICKEN OR FRIED TURKEY?
⁼GASP!⁼ BOTH!
DO WE WANT COCOA CRUNCHIES OR SUGAR SNAPS?
BOTH! BOTH! BOTH!
⁼BELCH!⁼ MAYBE WE SHOULDN'T HAVE HAD BOTH?
OF WHAT?
EVERYTHING!
LINCOLN! DAD'S HERE!
HEY, KIDDOS. WHAT SAY WE GET ICE CREAM ON THE WAY HOME?
⁼GROAN!⁼ ICE CREAM?!
WAS IS IT SOMETHING I SAID?
I GUESS THAT'S ONE MORE RULE ABOUT COLLEGE LIFE. NEVER GO TO THE CAFETERIA WITHOUT TO-GO BOXES!
BONK
BONK
BONK
END

"HOW YOU LIKE THEM APPLES?"

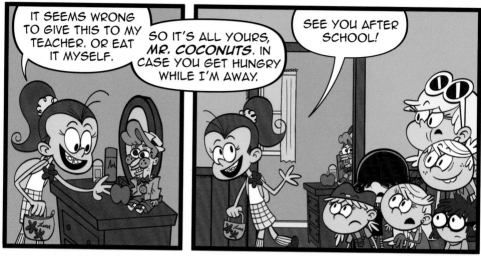

IT SEEMS WRONG TO GIVE THIS TO MY TEACHER. OR EAT IT MYSELF.

SO IT'S ALL YOURS, *MR. COCONUTS.* IN CASE YOU GET HUNGRY WHILE I'M AWAY.

SEE YOU AFTER SCHOOL!

BANANAS. TOO CHEERFUL.

DO YOU THINK HE LIKES ORANGES?

TAKE MY TAPIOCA PUDDING. YUCK!

WHAT HAVE WE HERE?

JACKPOT!

SO HOW WAS SCHOOL...?

WHOA, IT'S GONE! DID YOUR DOLL EAT ALL OUR FOOD?

NAH. MR. COCONUTS JUST FEEDS ON ATTENTION!

CLEARLY THERE'S GOT TO BE A SCIENTIFIC EXPLANATION FOR THIS.

BURP!

END

24

"IT SUITS YOU"

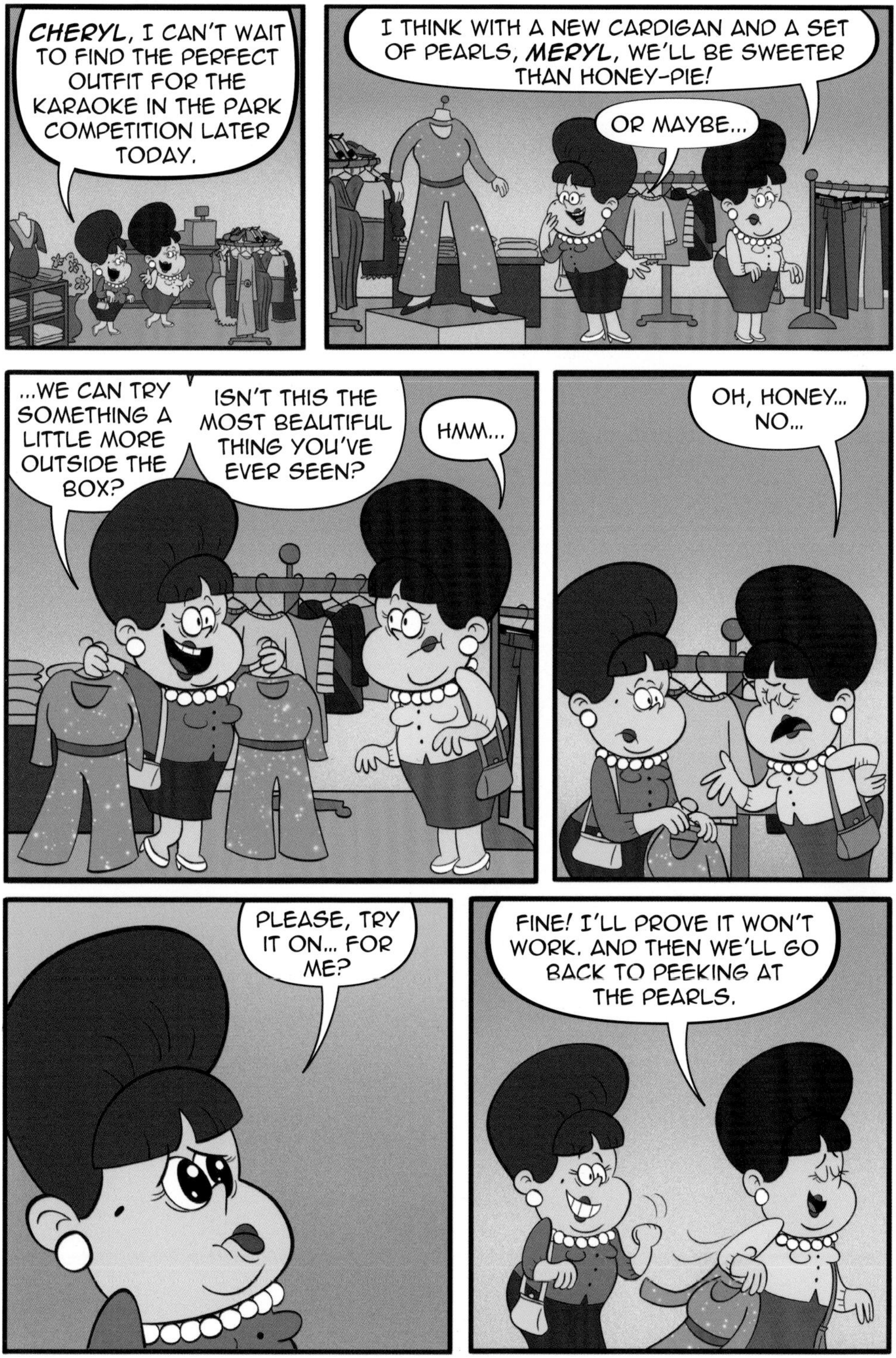
CHERYL, I CAN'T WAIT TO FIND THE PERFECT OUTFIT FOR THE KARAOKE IN THE PARK COMPETITION LATER TODAY.
I THINK WITH A NEW CARDIGAN AND A SET OF PEARLS, MERYL, WE'LL BE SWEETER THAN HONEY-PIE!
OR MAYBE...
...WE CAN TRY SOMETHING A LITTLE MORE OUTSIDE THE BOX?
ISN'T THIS THE MOST BEAUTIFUL THING YOU'VE EVER SEEN?
HMM...
OH, HONEY... NO...
PLEASE, TRY IT ON... FOR ME?
FINE! I'LL PROVE IT WON'T WORK. AND THEN WE'LL GO BACK TO PEEKING AT THE PEARLS.

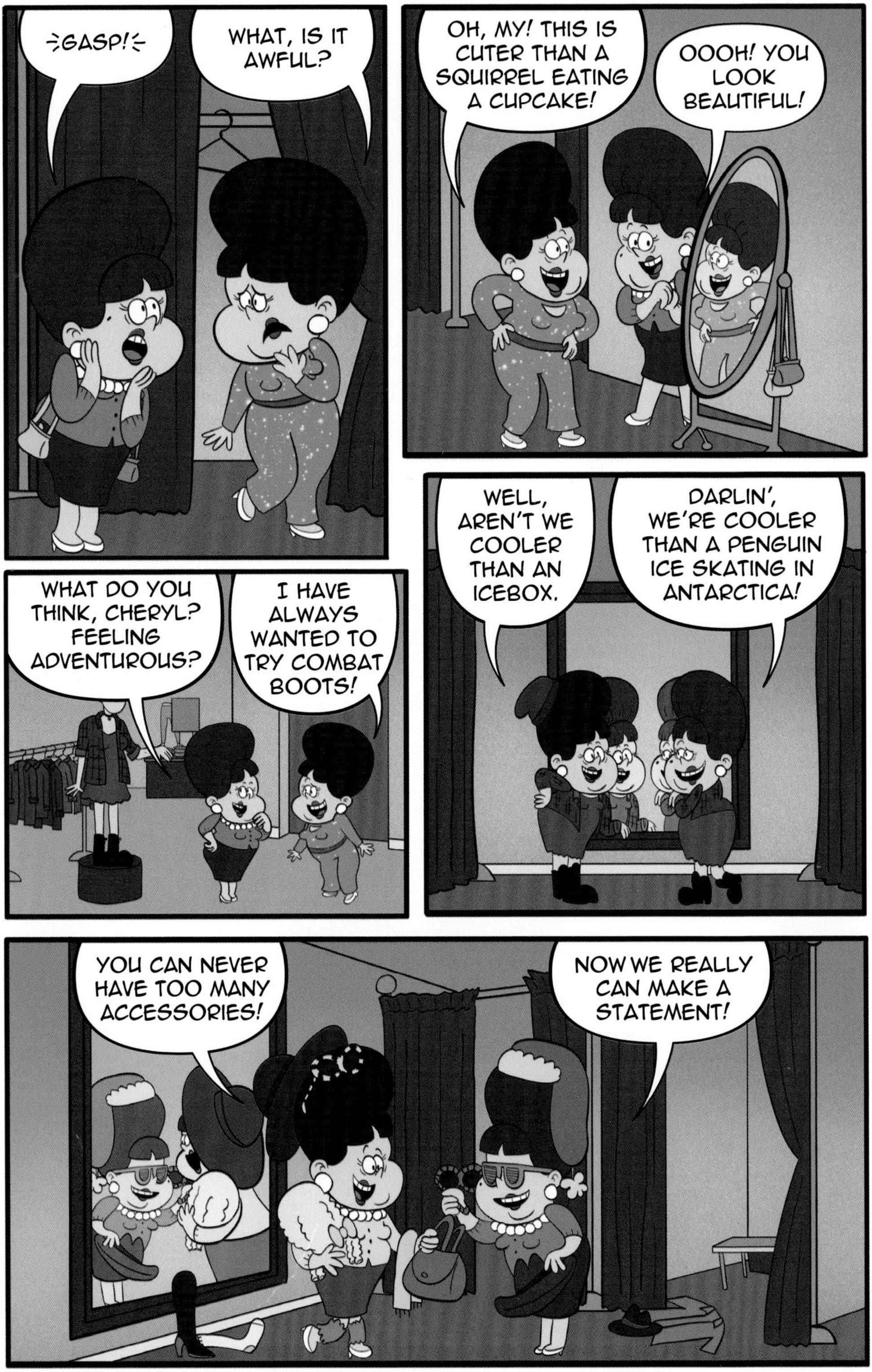
GASP!
WHAT, IS IT AWFUL?
OH, MY! THIS IS CUTER THAN A SQUIRREL EATING A CUPCAKE!
OOOH! YOU LOOK BEAUTIFUL!
WHAT DO YOU THINK, CHERYL? FEELING ADVENTUROUS?
I HAVE ALWAYS WANTED TO TRY COMBAT BOOTS!
WELL, AREN'T WE COOLER THAN AN ICEBOX.
DARLIN', WE'RE COOLER THAN A PENGUIN ICE SKATING IN ANTARCTICA!
YOU CAN NEVER HAVE TOO MANY ACCESSORIES!
NOW WE REALLY CAN MAKE A STATEMENT!

WHO KNEW THE POWDERED WIG COULD FRAME MY FACE SO WELL?

WE HAVE TO KEEP THESE STYLES IN MIND AT OUR NEXT HAIRCUT!

DO I LOOK READY TO ROAR?

BETTER SAVE THESE FOR NEXT MONTH'S KARAOKE COMPETITION AT THE ZOO!

÷OOF!÷ I THINK WE'RE RUNNING OUT OF TIME.

YEAH, LET'S GET SERIOUS.

IS IT BAD LUCK TO WEAR WHITE TO A KARAOKE COMPETITION?

BETTER NOT RISK IT!

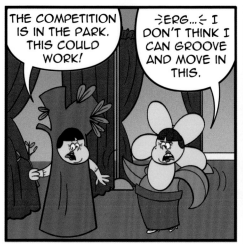

THE COMPETITION IS IN THE PARK. THIS COULD WORK!

÷ERG...÷ I DON'T THINK I CAN GROOVE AND MOVE IN THIS.

YOU WERE RIGHT ALL ALONG, SUGAR!

THANKS, CHER-BEAR! LET'S GET THESE CUTE CABOOSES TO THE PARK!

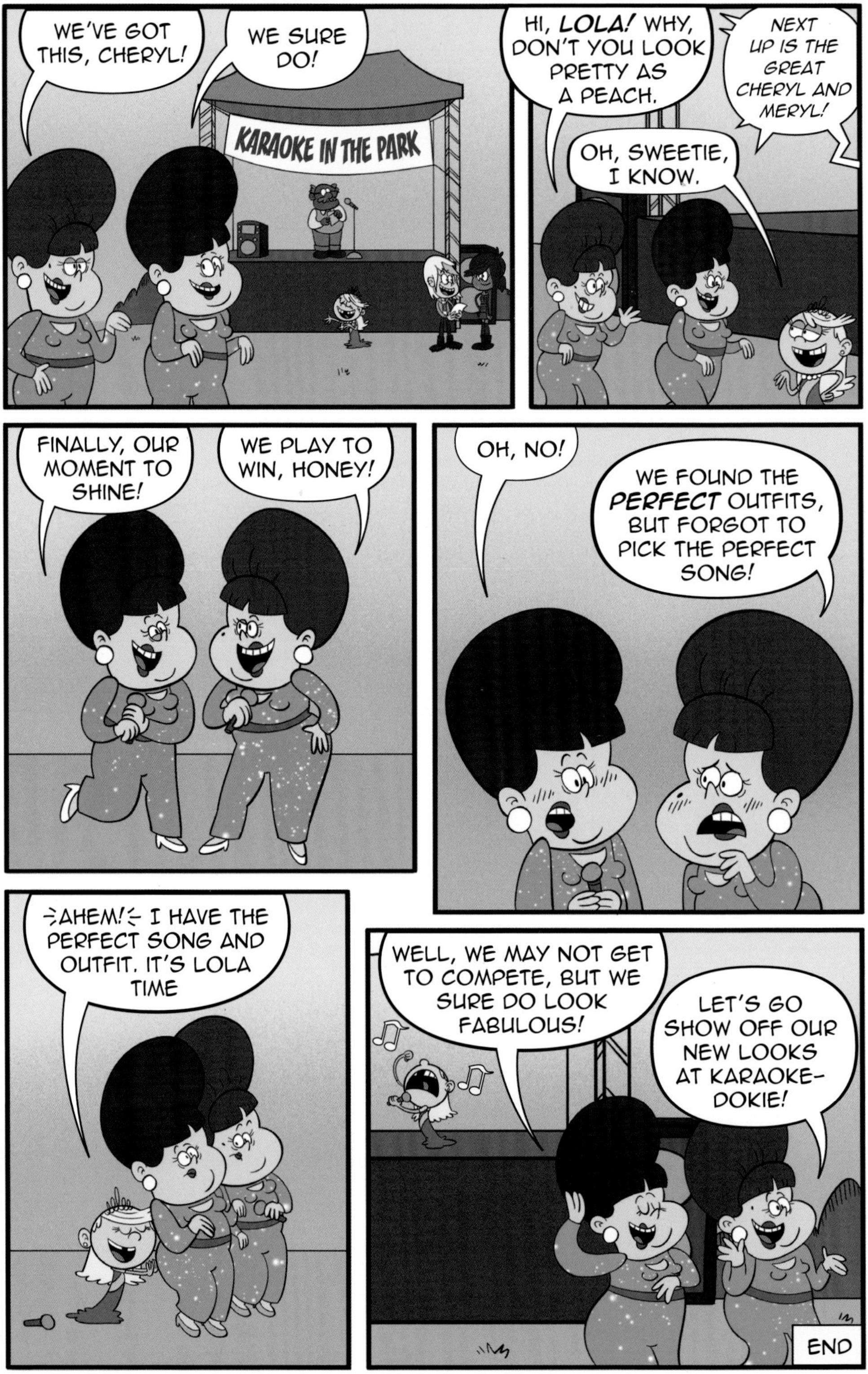
WE'VE GOT THIS, CHERYL!
WE SURE DO!
KARAOKE IN THE PARK
HI, LOLA! WHY, DON'T YOU LOOK PRETTY AS A PEACH.
NEXT UP IS THE GREAT CHERYL AND MERYL!
OH, SWEETIE, I KNOW.
FINALLY, OUR MOMENT TO SHINE!
WE PLAY TO WIN, HONEY!
OH, NO!
WE FOUND THE PERFECT OUTFITS, BUT FORGOT TO PICK THE PERFECT SONG!
AHEM! I HAVE THE PERFECT SONG AND OUTFIT. IT'S LOLA TIME
WELL, WE MAY NOT GET TO COMPETE, BUT WE SURE DO LOOK FABULOUS!
LET'S GO SHOW OFF OUR NEW LOOKS AT KARAOKE-DOKIE!
END

"PARADE OF FOOLS"

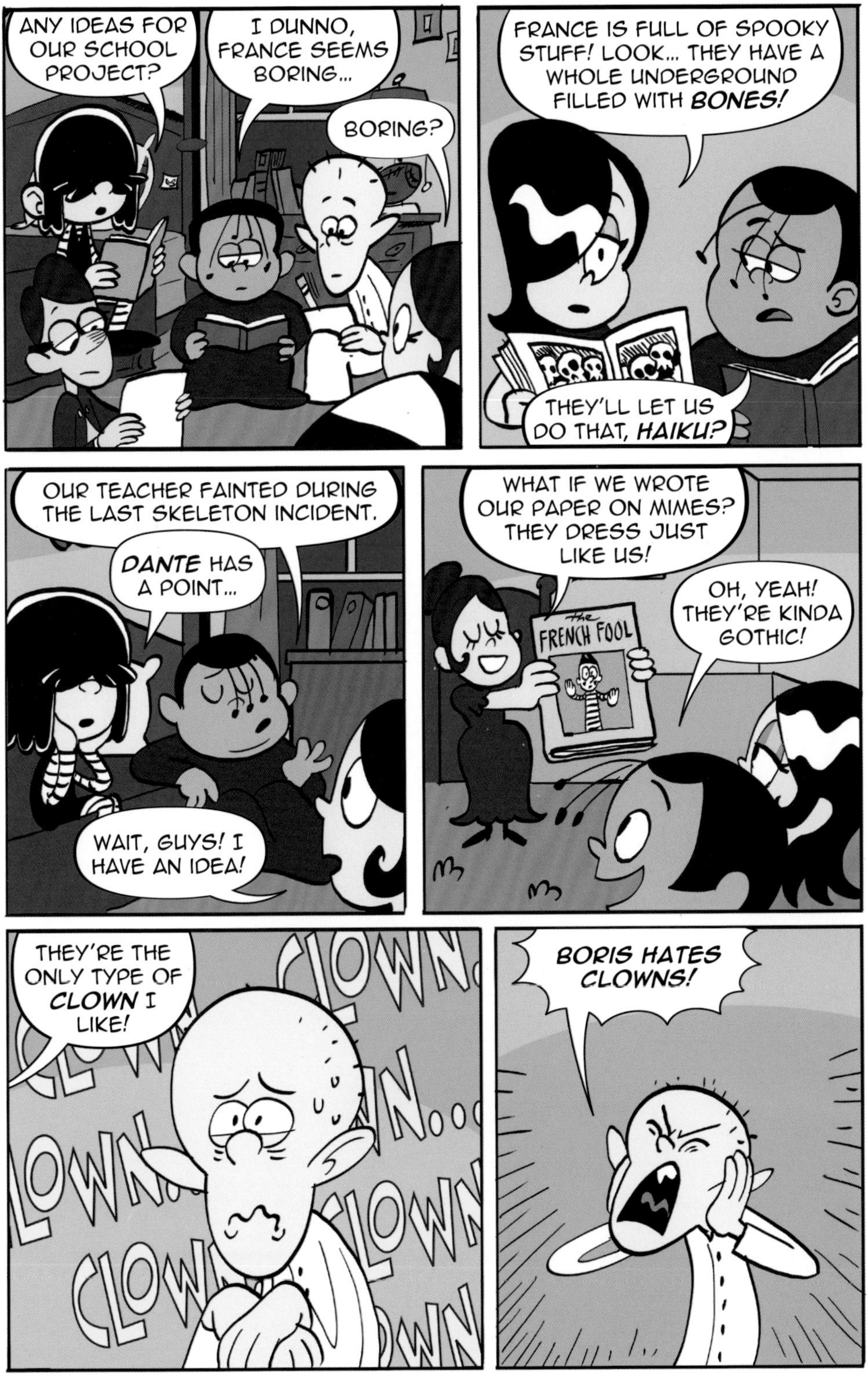

ANY IDEAS FOR OUR SCHOOL PROJECT?
I DUNNO, FRANCE SEEMS BORING...
BORING?
FRANCE IS FULL OF SPOOKY STUFF! LOOK... THEY HAVE A WHOLE UNDERGROUND FILLED WITH BONES!
THEY'LL LET US DO THAT, HAIKU?
OUR TEACHER FAINTED DURING THE LAST SKELETON INCIDENT.
DANTE HAS A POINT...
WAIT, GUYS! I HAVE AN IDEA!
WHAT IF WE WROTE OUR PAPER ON MIMES? THEY DRESS JUST LIKE US!
The FRENCH FOOL
OH, YEAH! THEY'RE KINDA GOTHIC!
THEY'RE THE ONLY TYPE OF CLOWN I LIKE!
BORIS HATES CLOWNS!

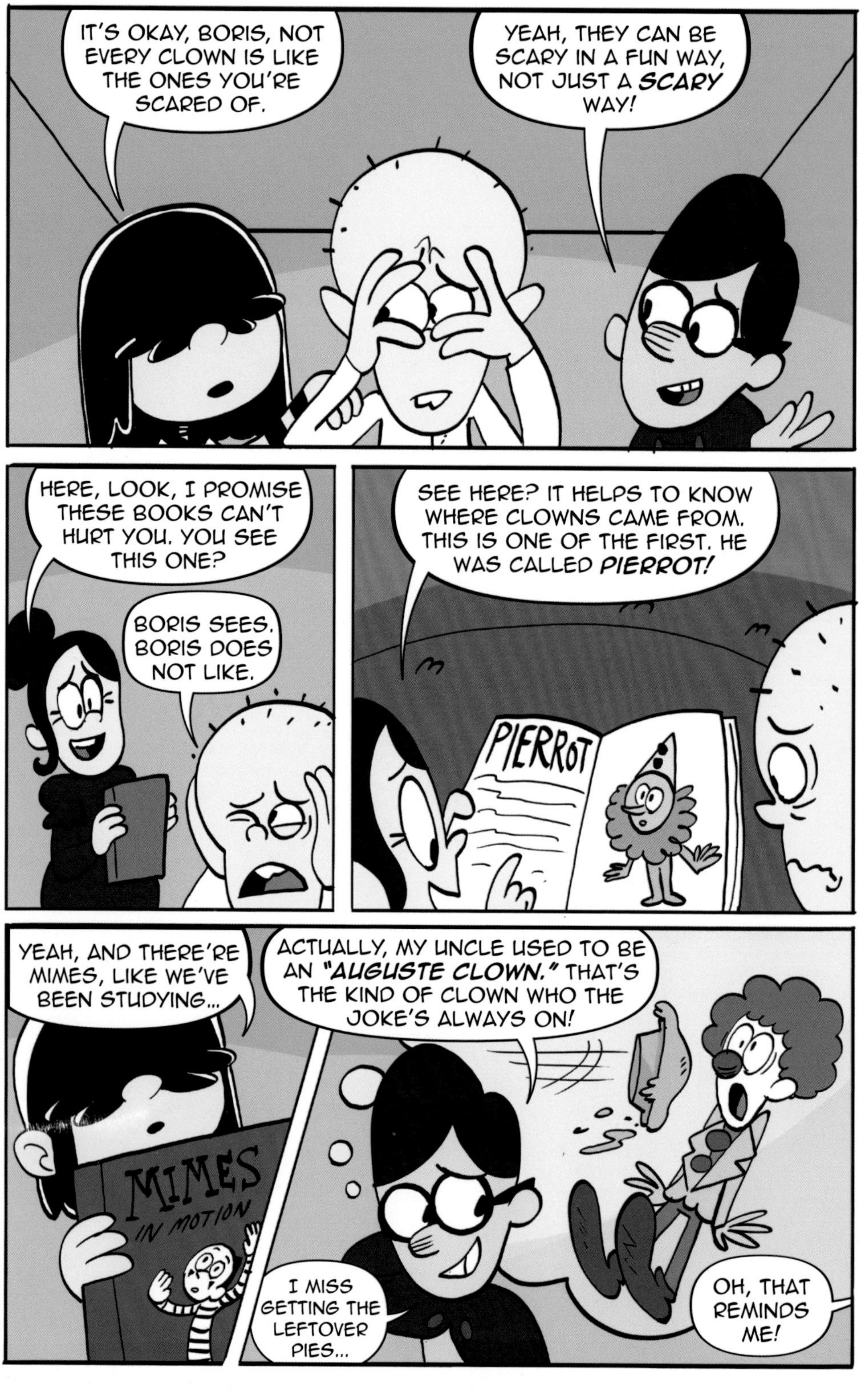
IT'S OKAY, BORIS, NOT EVERY CLOWN IS LIKE THE ONES YOU'RE SCARED OF.
YEAH, THEY CAN BE SCARY IN A FUN WAY, NOT JUST A *SCARY* WAY!
HERE, LOOK, I PROMISE THESE BOOKS CAN'T HURT YOU. YOU SEE THIS ONE?
BORIS SEES. BORIS DOES NOT LIKE.
SEE HERE? IT HELPS TO KNOW WHERE CLOWNS CAME FROM. THIS IS ONE OF THE FIRST. HE WAS CALLED *PIERROT!*
PIERROT
YEAH, AND THERE'RE MIMES, LIKE WE'VE BEEN STUDYING...
MIMES IN MOTION
ACTUALLY, MY UNCLE USED TO BE AN *"AUGUSTE CLOWN."* THAT'S THE KIND OF CLOWN WHO THE JOKE'S ALWAYS ON!
I MISS GETTING THE LEFTOVER PIES...
OH, THAT REMINDS ME!

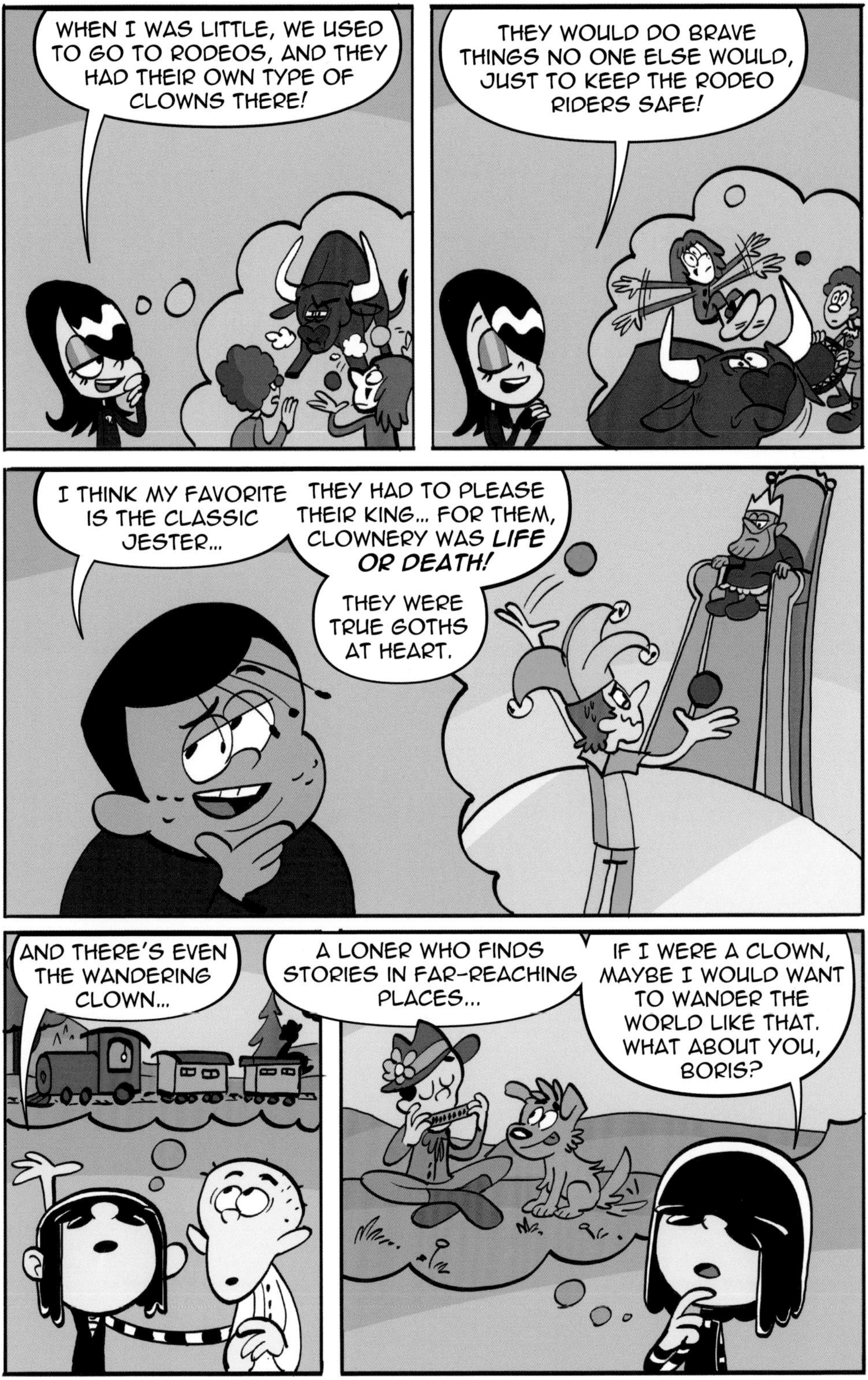
WHEN I WAS LITTLE, WE USED TO GO TO RODEOS, AND THEY HAD THEIR OWN TYPE OF CLOWNS THERE!
THEY WOULD DO BRAVE THINGS NO ONE ELSE WOULD, JUST TO KEEP THE RODEO RIDERS SAFE!
I THINK MY FAVORITE IS THE CLASSIC JESTER...
THEY HAD TO PLEASE THEIR KING... FOR THEM, CLOWNERY WAS ***LIFE OR DEATH!***
THEY WERE TRUE GOTHS AT HEART.
AND THERE'S EVEN THE WANDERING CLOWN...
A LONER WHO FINDS STORIES IN FAR-REACHING PLACES...
IF I WERE A CLOWN, MAYBE I WOULD WANT TO WANDER THE WORLD LIKE THAT. WHAT ABOUT YOU, BORIS?

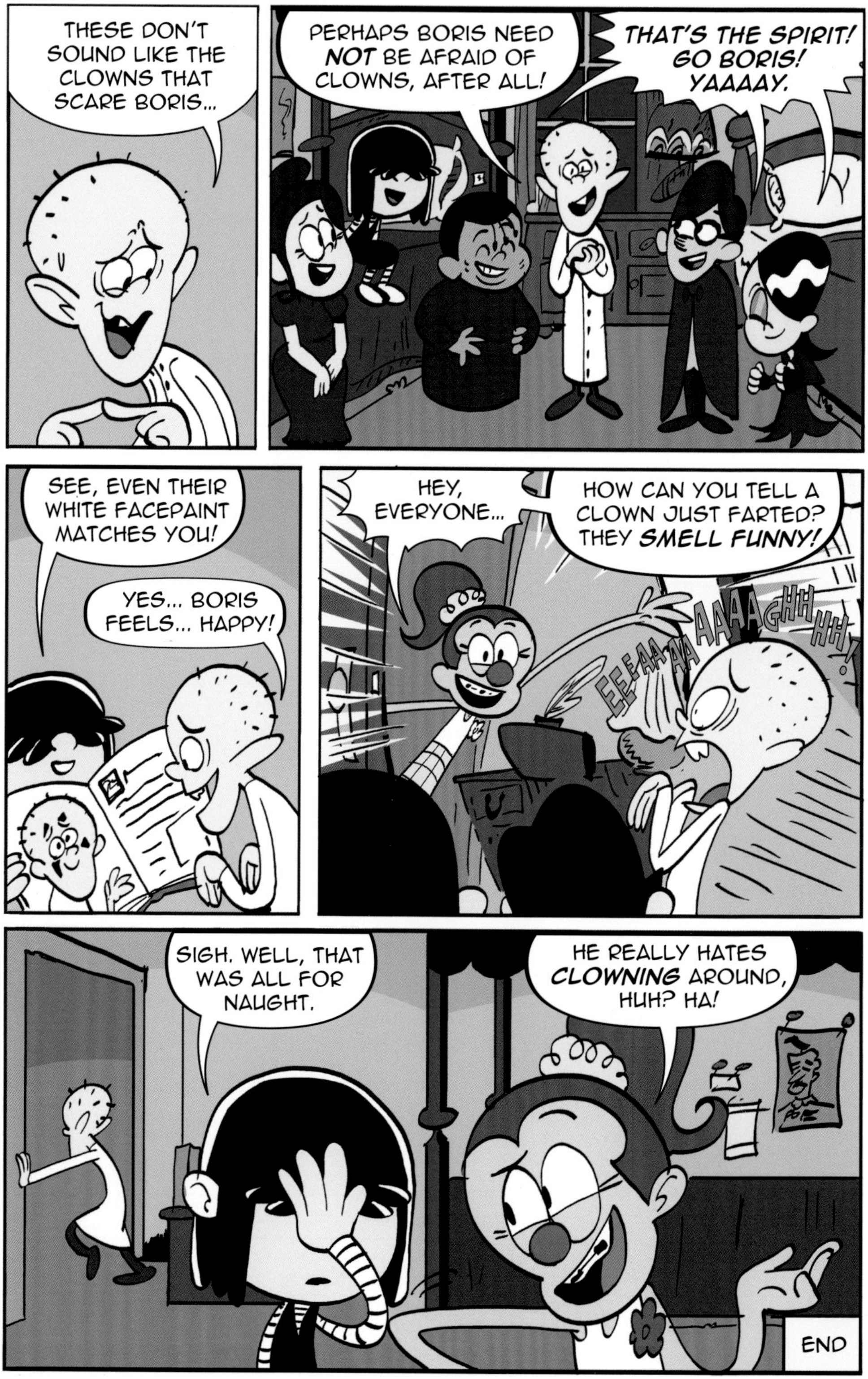
THESE DON'T SOUND LIKE THE CLOWNS THAT SCARE BORIS...
PERHAPS BORIS NEED **NOT** BE AFRAID OF CLOWNS, AFTER ALL!
THAT'S THE SPIRIT! GO BORIS! YAAAAY.
SEE, EVEN THEIR WHITE FACEPAINT MATCHES YOU!
YES... BORIS FEELS... HAPPY!
HEY, EVERYONE...
HOW CAN YOU TELL A CLOWN JUST FARTED? THEY **SMELL FUNNY!**
EEEAAAAAAAAAGHHHHH!
SIGH. WELL, THAT WAS ALL FOR NAUGHT.
HE REALLY HATES **CLOWNING** AROUND, HUH? HA!
END

"PASS CLASS OR DASH"

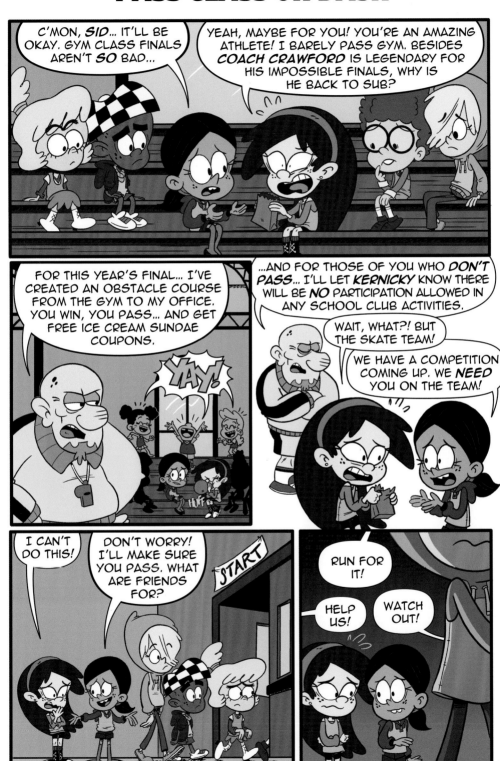

C'MON, **SID**... IT'LL BE OKAY. GYM CLASS FINALS AREN'T **SO** BAD...

YEAH, MAYBE FOR YOU! YOU'RE AN AMAZING ATHLETE! I BARELY PASS GYM. BESIDES **COACH CRAWFORD** IS LEGENDARY FOR HIS IMPOSSIBLE FINALS, WHY IS HE BACK TO SUB?

FOR THIS YEAR'S FINAL... I'VE CREATED AN OBSTACLE COURSE FROM THE GYM TO MY OFFICE. YOU WIN, YOU PASS... AND GET FREE ICE CREAM SUNDAE COUPONS.

YAY!

HUFF

...AND FOR THOSE OF YOU WHO **DON'T PASS**... I'LL LET **KERNICKY** KNOW THERE WILL BE **NO** PARTICIPATION ALLOWED IN ANY SCHOOL CLUB ACTIVITIES.

WAIT, WHAT?! BUT THE SKATE TEAM!

WE HAVE A COMPETITION COMING UP. WE **NEED** YOU ON THE TEAM!

I CAN'T DO THIS!

DON'T WORRY! I'LL MAKE SURE YOU PASS. WHAT ARE FRIENDS FOR?

START

RUN FOR IT!

HELP US!

WATCH OUT!

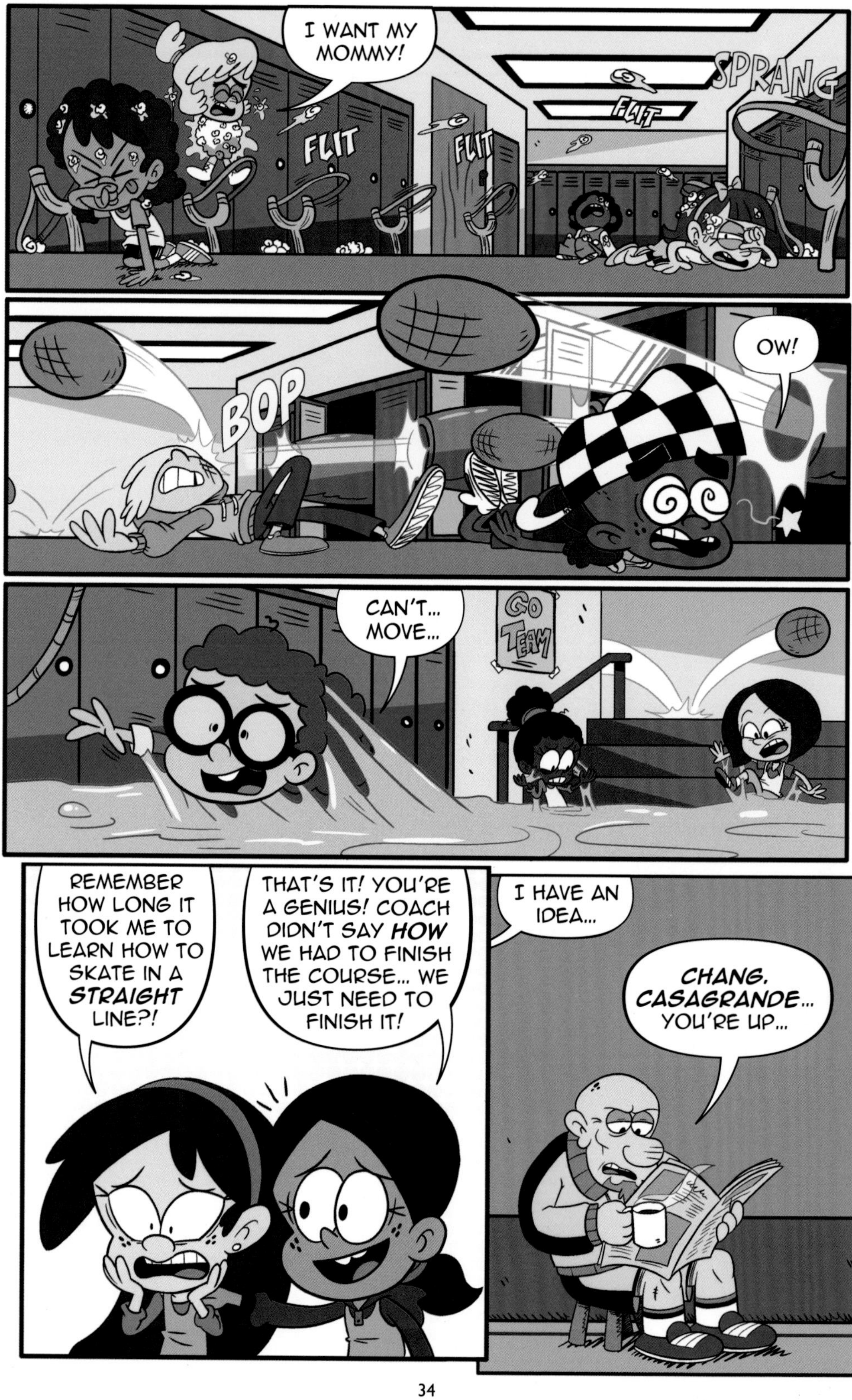

I WANT MY MOMMY!
SPRANG
FLIT
FLIT
FLIT
BOP
OW!
CAN'T... MOVE...
GO TEAM
REMEMBER HOW LONG IT TOOK ME TO LEARN HOW TO SKATE IN A STRAIGHT LINE?!
THAT'S IT! YOU'RE A GENIUS! COACH DIDN'T SAY HOW WE HAD TO FINISH THE COURSE... WE JUST NEED TO FINISH IT!
I HAVE AN IDEA...
CHANG. CASAGRANDE... YOU'RE UP...

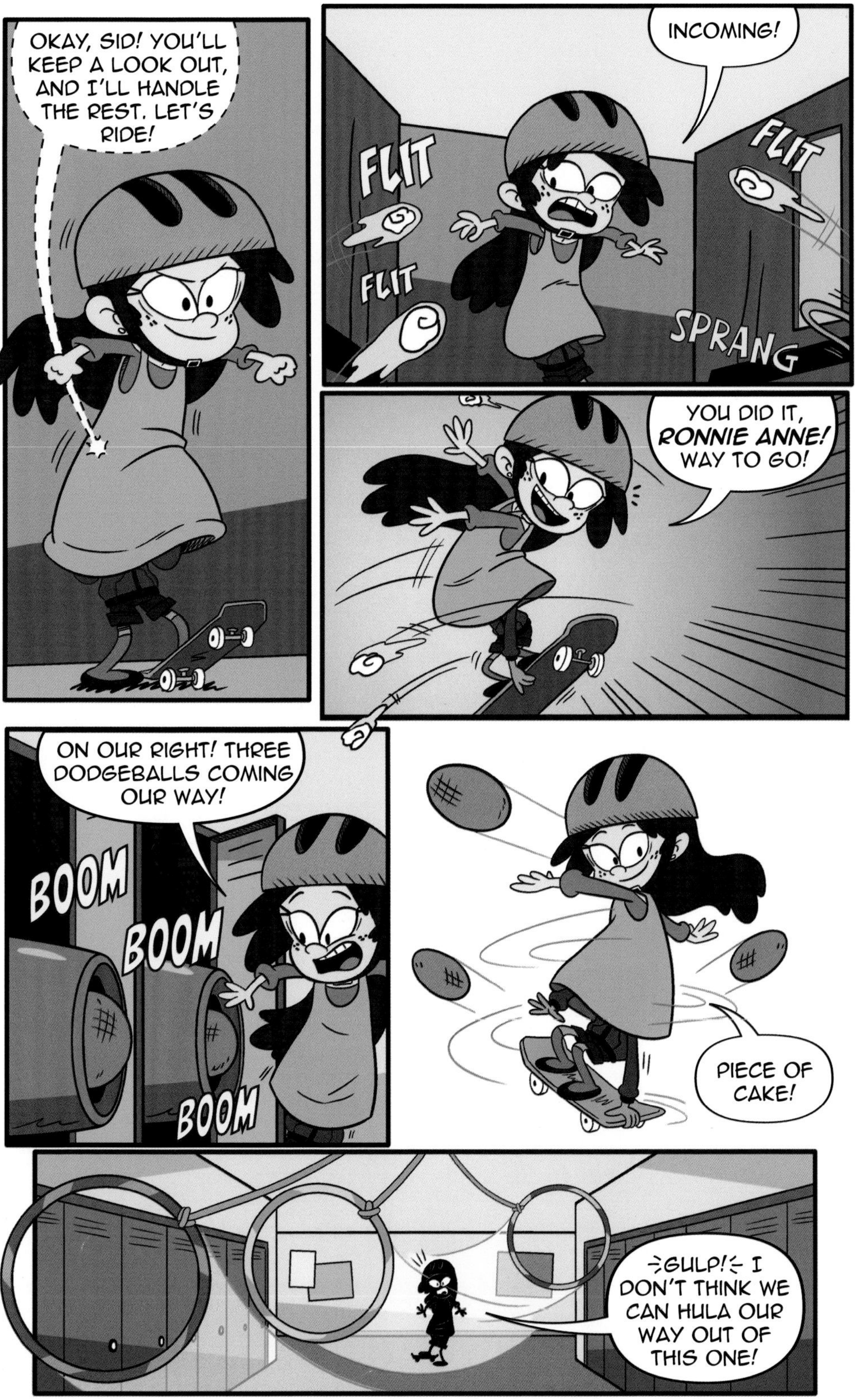
OKAY, SID! YOU'LL KEEP A LOOK OUT, AND I'LL HANDLE THE REST. LET'S RIDE!
INCOMING!
FLIT
FLIT
FLIT
SPRANG
YOU DID IT, RONNIE ANNE! WAY TO GO!
ON OUR RIGHT! THREE DODGEBALLS COMING OUR WAY!
BOOM
BOOM
BOOM
PIECE OF CAKE!
GULP! I DON'T THINK WE CAN HULA OUR WAY OUT OF THIS ONE!

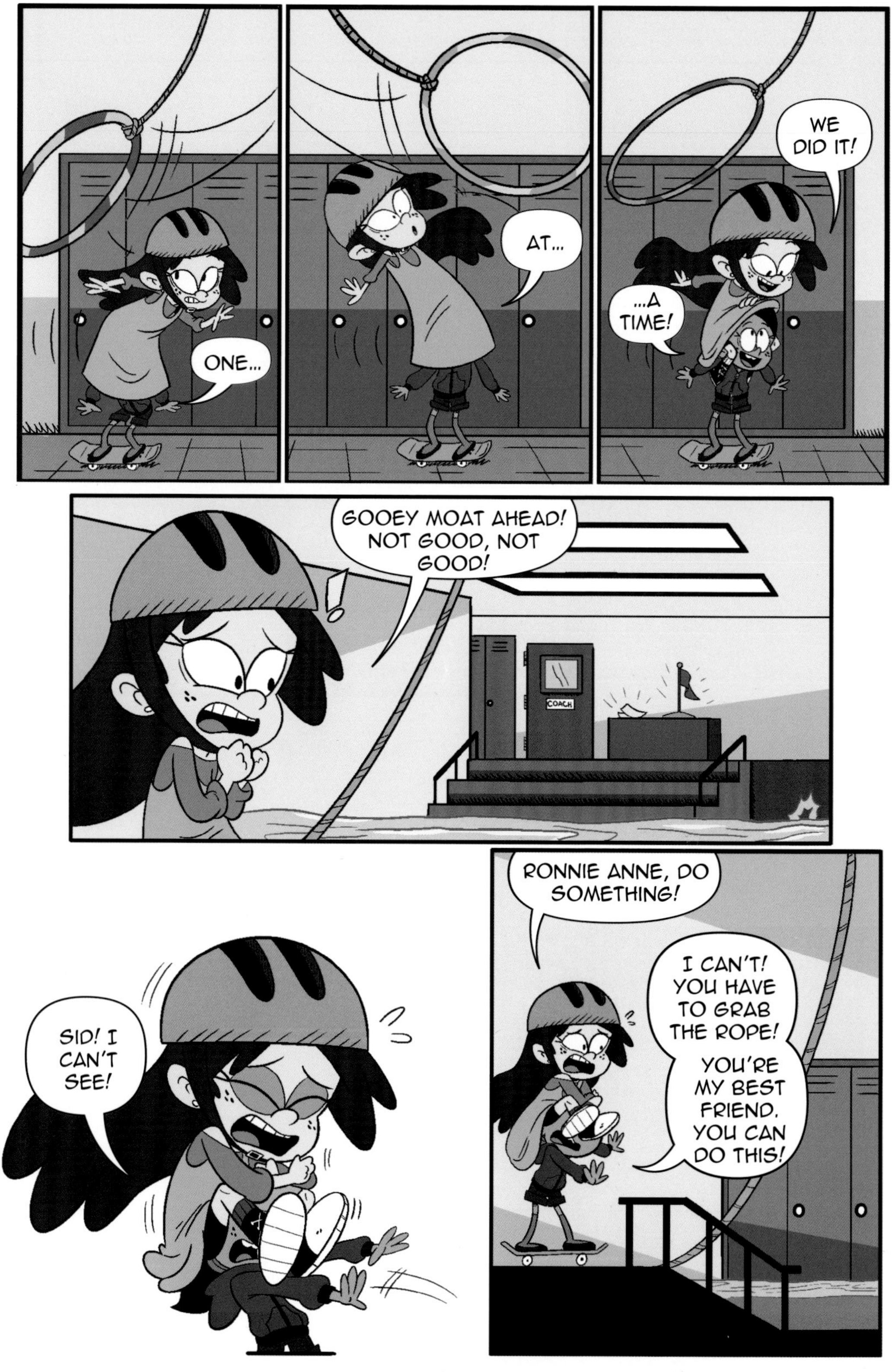
ONE...
AT...
...A TIME!
WE DID IT!
GOOEY MOAT AHEAD! NOT GOOD, NOT GOOD!
COACH
SID! I CAN'T SEE!
RONNIE ANNE, DO SOMETHING!
I CAN'T! YOU HAVE TO GRAB THE ROPE!
YOU'RE MY BEST FRIEND. YOU CAN DO THIS!

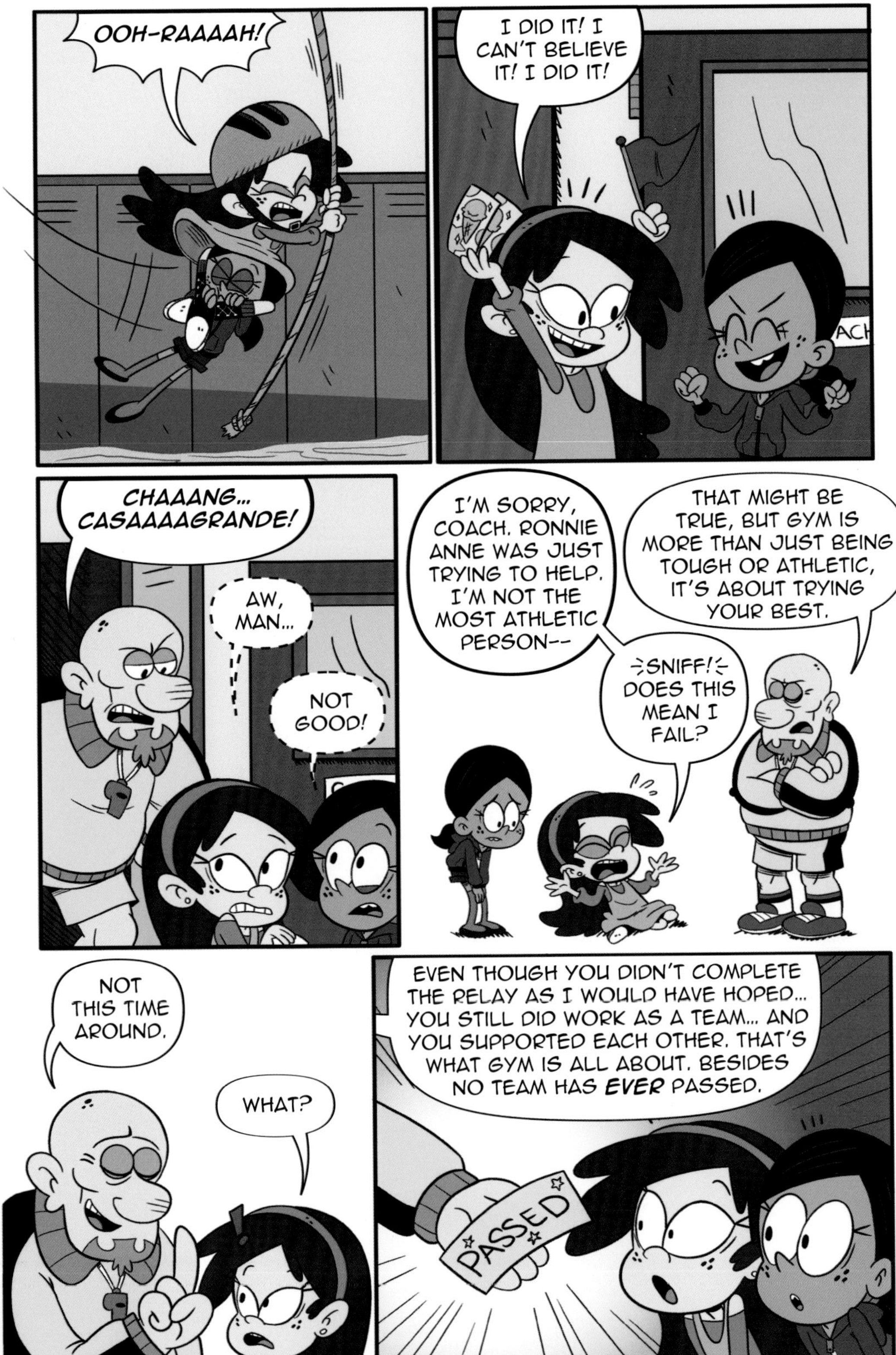
OOH-RAAAAH!
I DID IT! I CAN'T BELIEVE IT! I DID IT!
CHAAANG... CASAAAAGRANDE!
AW, MAN...
NOT GOOD!
I'M SORRY, COACH. RONNIE ANNE WAS JUST TRYING TO HELP. I'M NOT THE MOST ATHLETIC PERSON--
SNIFF! DOES THIS MEAN I FAIL?
THAT MIGHT BE TRUE, BUT GYM IS MORE THAN JUST BEING TOUGH OR ATHLETIC, IT'S ABOUT TRYING YOUR BEST.
NOT THIS TIME AROUND.
WHAT?
EVEN THOUGH YOU DIDN'T COMPLETE THE RELAY AS I WOULD HAVE HOPED... YOU STILL DID WORK AS A TEAM... AND YOU SUPPORTED EACH OTHER. THAT'S WHAT GYM IS ALL ABOUT. BESIDES NO TEAM HAS ***EVER*** PASSED.
PASSED

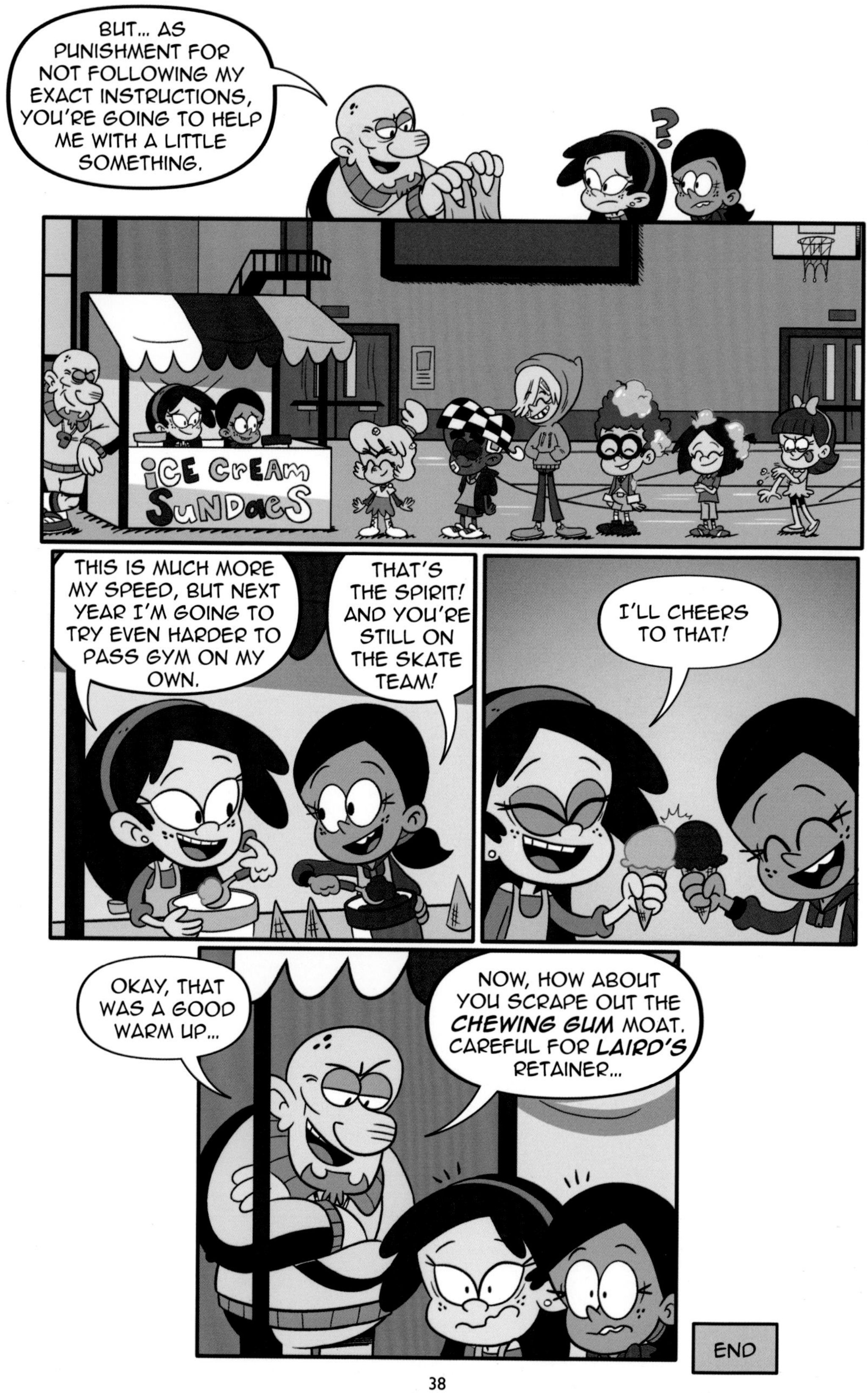
BUT... AS PUNISHMENT FOR NOT FOLLOWING MY EXACT INSTRUCTIONS, YOU'RE GOING TO HELP ME WITH A LITTLE SOMETHING.
?
ICE CREAM SUNDAES
THIS IS MUCH MORE MY SPEED, BUT NEXT YEAR I'M GOING TO TRY EVEN HARDER TO PASS GYM ON MY OWN.
THAT'S THE SPIRIT! AND YOU'RE STILL ON THE SKATE TEAM!
I'LL CHEERS TO THAT!
OKAY, THAT WAS A GOOD WARM UP...
NOW, HOW ABOUT YOU SCRAPE OUT THE CHEWING GUM MOAT. CAREFUL FOR LAIRD'S RETAINER...
END

"EXCHANGE OF PACE!"

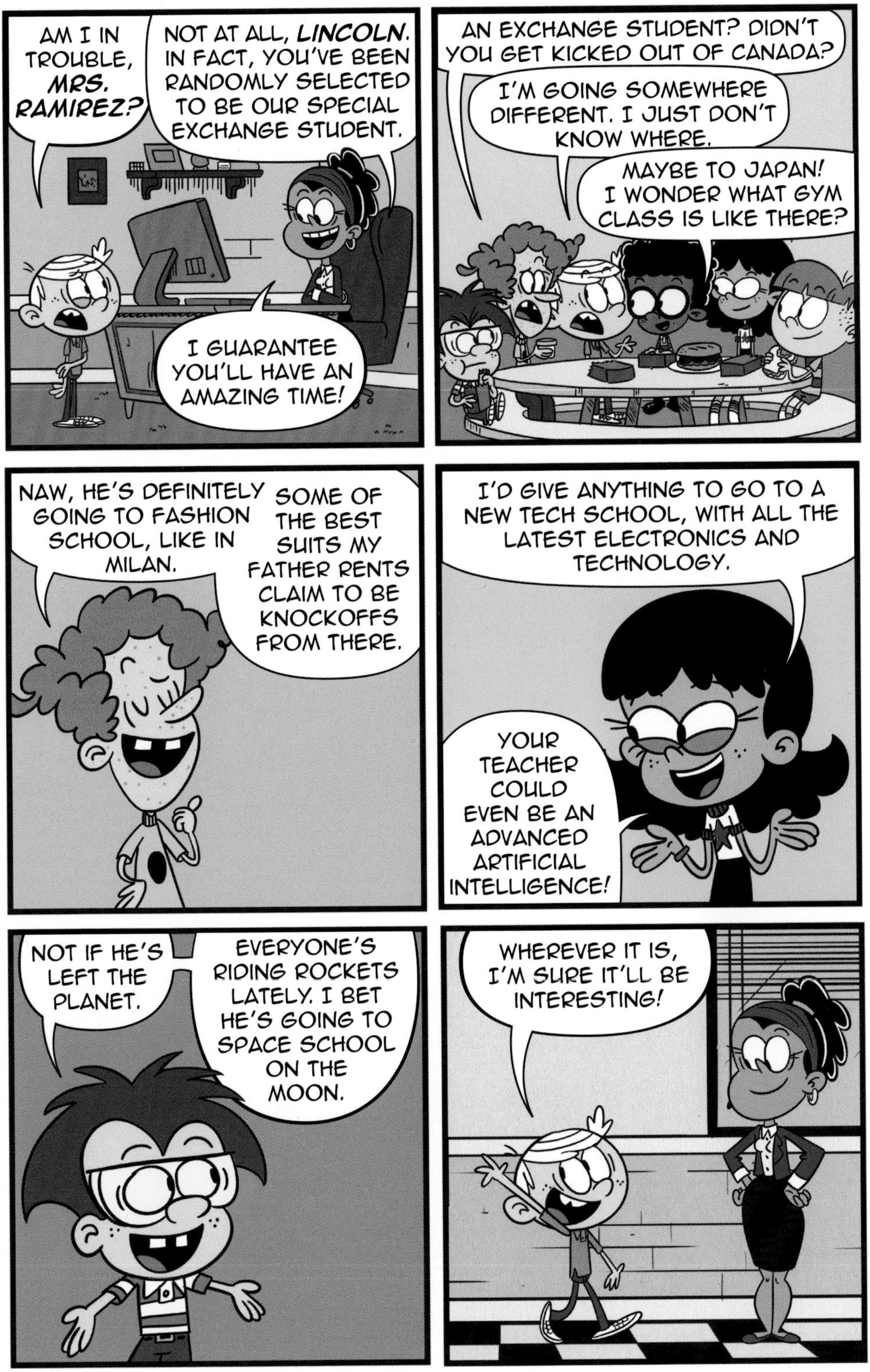
AM I IN TROUBLE, MRS. RAMIREZ?
NOT AT ALL, LINCOLN. IN FACT, YOU'VE BEEN RANDOMLY SELECTED TO BE OUR SPECIAL EXCHANGE STUDENT.
I GUARANTEE YOU'LL HAVE AN AMAZING TIME!
AN EXCHANGE STUDENT? DIDN'T YOU GET KICKED OUT OF CANADA?
I'M GOING SOMEWHERE DIFFERENT. I JUST DON'T KNOW WHERE.
MAYBE TO JAPAN! I WONDER WHAT GYM CLASS IS LIKE THERE?
NAW, HE'S DEFINITELY GOING TO FASHION SCHOOL, LIKE IN MILAN.
SOME OF THE BEST SUITS MY FATHER RENTS CLAIM TO BE KNOCKOFFS FROM THERE.
I'D GIVE ANYTHING TO GO TO A NEW TECH SCHOOL, WITH ALL THE LATEST ELECTRONICS AND TECHNOLOGY.
YOUR TEACHER COULD EVEN BE AN ADVANCED ARTIFICIAL INTELLIGENCE!
NOT IF HE'S LEFT THE PLANET.
EVERYONE'S RIDING ROCKETS LATELY. I BET HE'S GOING TO SPACE SCHOOL ON THE MOON.
WHEREVER IT IS, I'M SURE IT'LL BE INTERESTING!

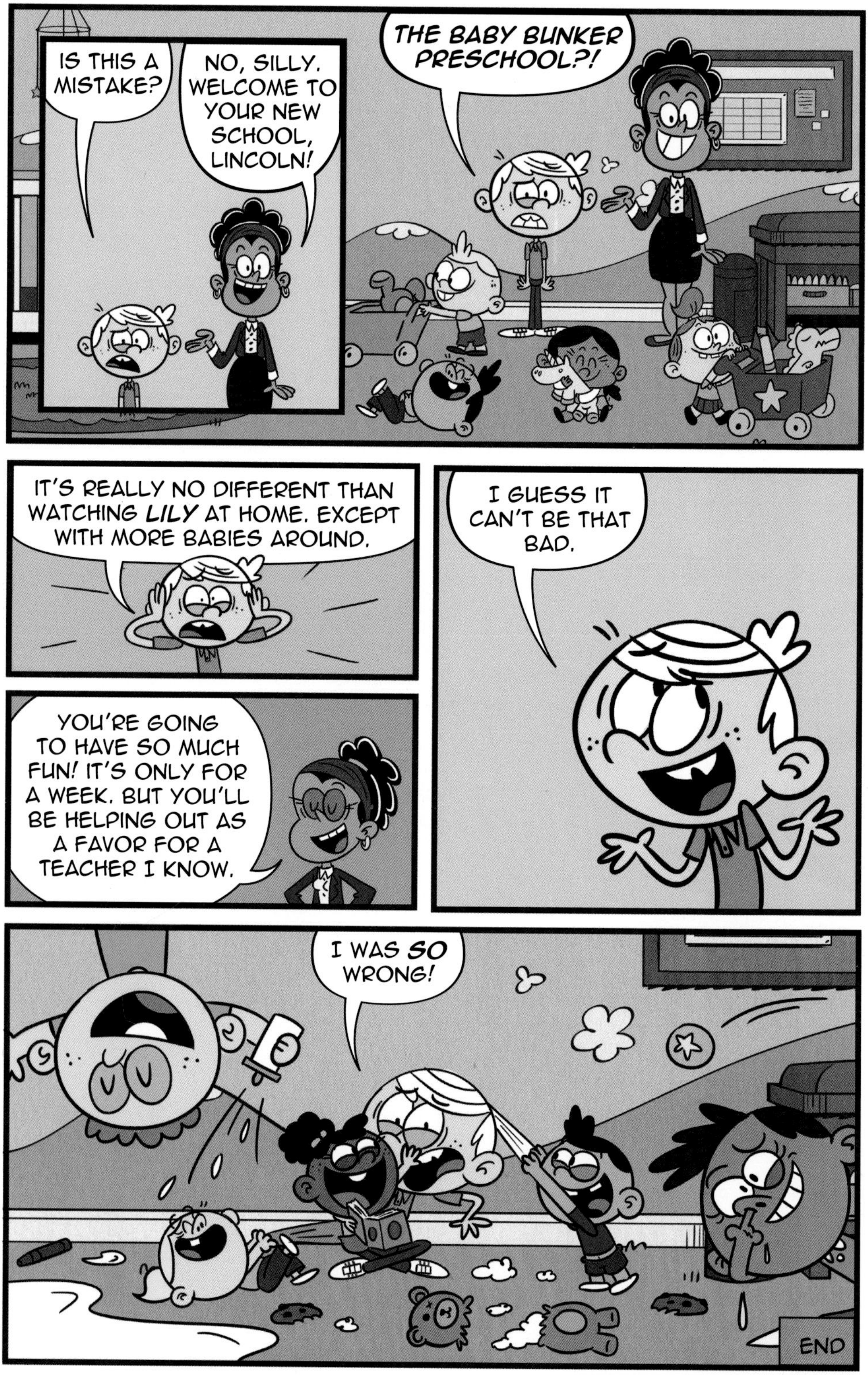
IS THIS A MISTAKE?
NO, SILLY. WELCOME TO YOUR NEW SCHOOL, LINCOLN!
THE BABY BUNKER PRESCHOOL?!
IT'S REALLY NO DIFFERENT THAN WATCHING LILY AT HOME. EXCEPT WITH MORE BABIES AROUND.
YOU'RE GOING TO HAVE SO MUCH FUN! IT'S ONLY FOR A WEEK. BUT YOU'LL BE HELPING OUT AS A FAVOR FOR A TEACHER I KNOW.
I GUESS IT CAN'T BE THAT BAD.
I WAS SO WRONG!
END

"TRAILER PORK"

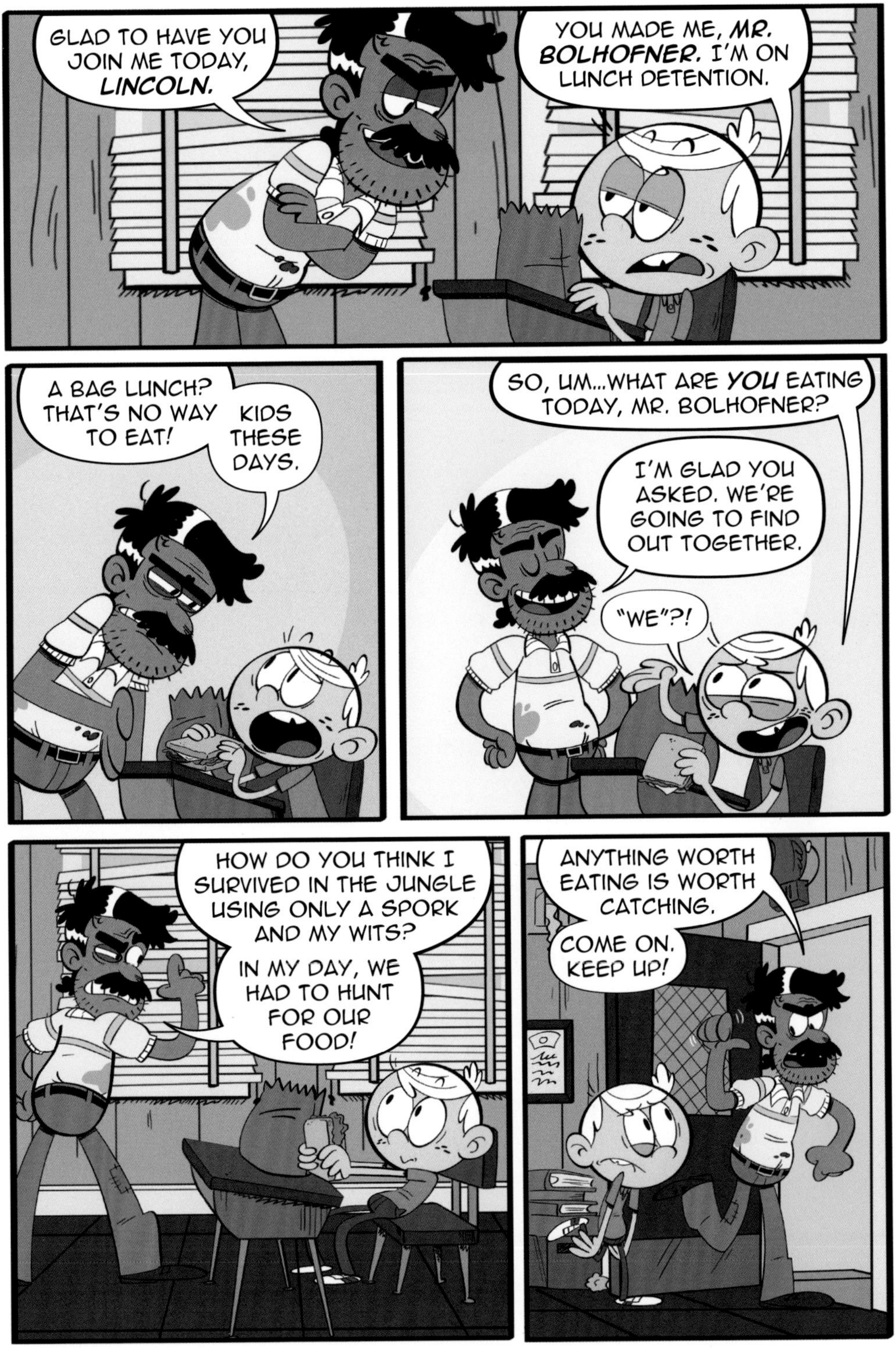
GLAD TO HAVE YOU JOIN ME TODAY, LINCOLN.
YOU MADE ME, MR. BOLHOFNER. I'M ON LUNCH DETENTION.
A BAG LUNCH? THAT'S NO WAY TO EAT!
KIDS THESE DAYS.
SO, UM...WHAT ARE YOU EATING TODAY, MR. BOLHOFNER?
I'M GLAD YOU ASKED. WE'RE GOING TO FIND OUT TOGETHER.
"WE"?!
HOW DO YOU THINK I SURVIVED IN THE JUNGLE USING ONLY A SPORK AND MY WITS?
IN MY DAY, WE HAD TO HUNT FOR OUR FOOD!
ANYTHING WORTH EATING IS WORTH CATCHING.
COME ON. KEEP UP!

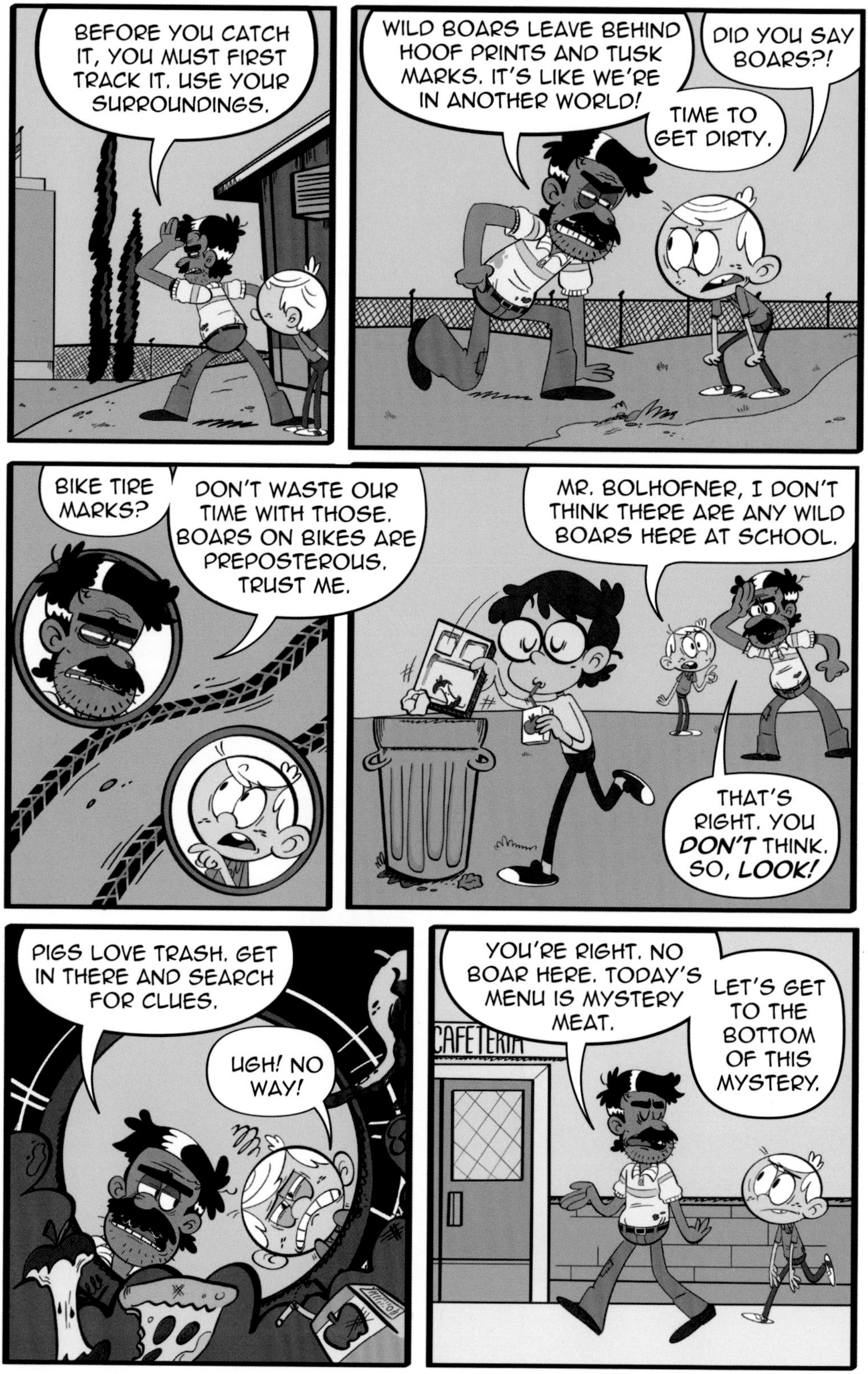
BEFORE YOU CATCH IT, YOU MUST FIRST TRACK IT. USE YOUR SURROUNDINGS.
WILD BOARS LEAVE BEHIND HOOF PRINTS AND TUSK MARKS. IT'S LIKE WE'RE IN ANOTHER WORLD!
DID YOU SAY BOARS?!
TIME TO GET DIRTY.
BIKE TIRE MARKS?
DON'T WASTE OUR TIME WITH THOSE. BOARS ON BIKES ARE PREPOSTEROUS. TRUST ME.
MR. BOLHOFNER, I DON'T THINK THERE ARE ANY WILD BOARS HERE AT SCHOOL.
THAT'S RIGHT. YOU DON'T THINK. SO, LOOK!
PIGS LOVE TRASH. GET IN THERE AND SEARCH FOR CLUES.
UGH! NO WAY!
YOU'RE RIGHT. NO BOAR HERE. TODAY'S MENU IS MYSTERY MEAT.
CAFETERIA
LET'S GET TO THE BOTTOM OF THIS MYSTERY.

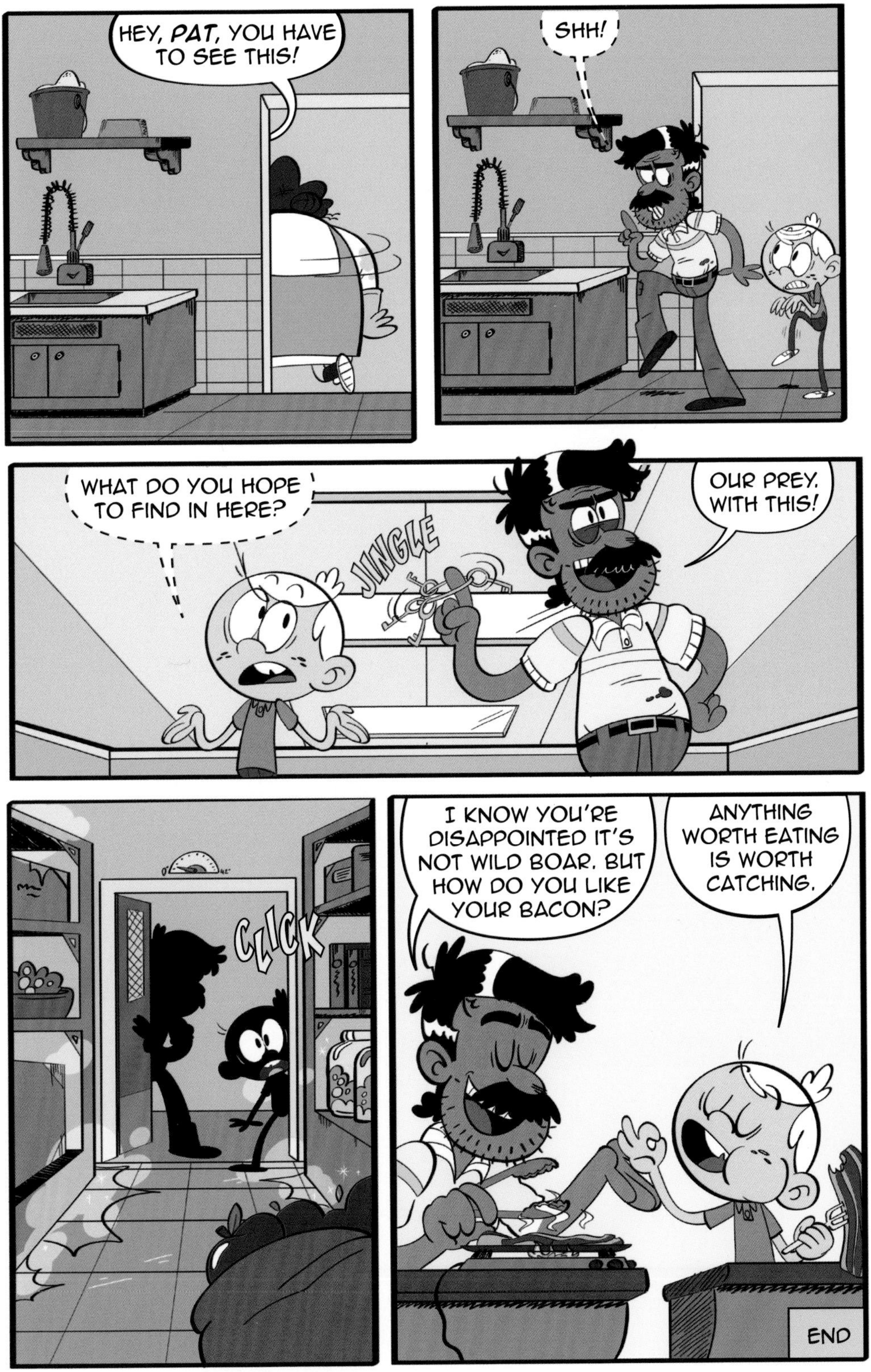
HEY, *PAT*, YOU HAVE TO SEE THIS!
SHH!
WHAT DO YOU HOPE TO FIND IN HERE?
JINGLE
OUR PREY. WITH THIS!
CLICK
I KNOW YOU'RE DISAPPOINTED IT'S NOT WILD BOAR. BUT HOW DO YOU LIKE YOUR BACON?
ANYTHING WORTH EATING IS WORTH CATCHING.
END

"STUDENT STORE LORE"

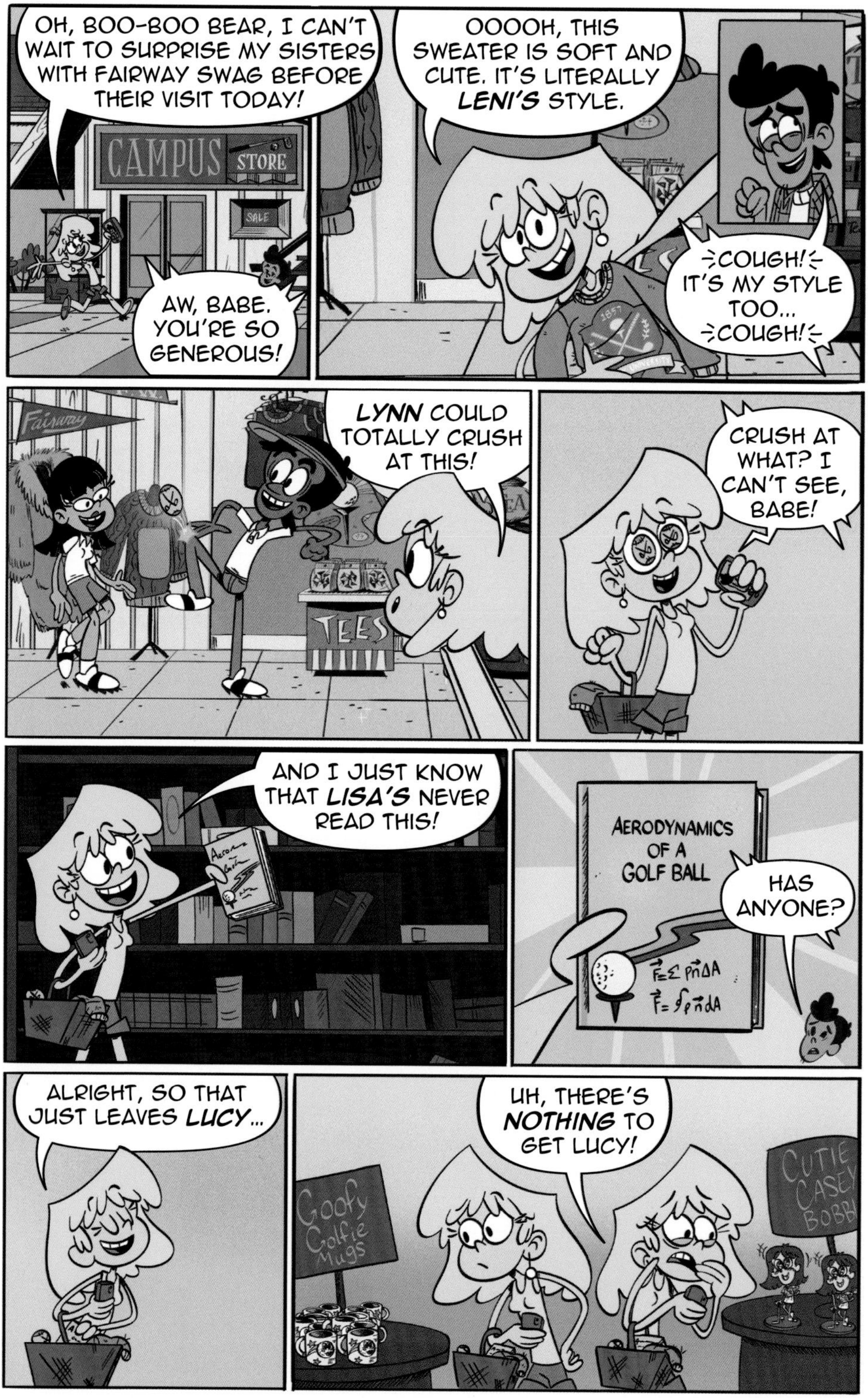

OH, BOO-BOO BEAR, I CAN'T WAIT TO SURPRISE MY SISTERS WITH FAIRWAY SWAG BEFORE THEIR VISIT TODAY!
CAMPUS STORE
SALE
AW, BABE. YOU'RE SO GENEROUS!
OOOOH, THIS SWEATER IS SOFT AND CUTE. IT'S LITERALLY LENI'S STYLE.
COUGH! IT'S MY STYLE TOO... COUGH!
Fairway
LYNN COULD TOTALLY CRUSH AT THIS!
TEES
CRUSH AT WHAT? I CAN'T SEE, BABE!
AND I JUST KNOW THAT LISA'S NEVER READ THIS!
AERODYNAMICS OF A GOLF BALL
HAS ANYONE?
ALRIGHT, SO THAT JUST LEAVES LUCY...
UH, THERE'S NOTHING TO GET LUCY!
Goofy Golfie Mugs
CUTIE CASEY BOBB

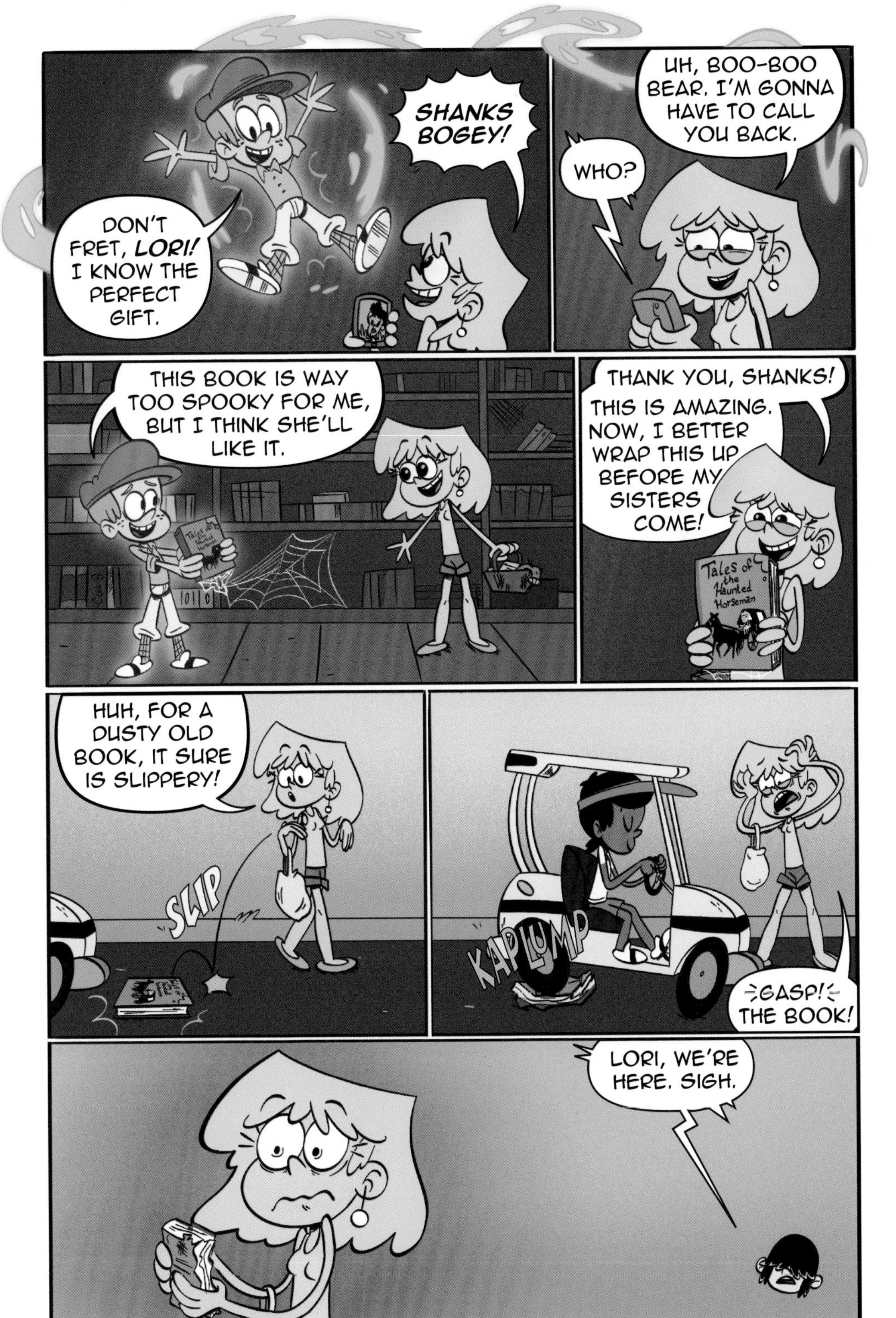
SHANKS BOGEY!
DON'T FRET, LORI! I KNOW THE PERFECT GIFT.
WHO?
UH, BOO-BOO BEAR. I'M GONNA HAVE TO CALL YOU BACK.
THIS BOOK IS WAY TOO SPOOKY FOR ME, BUT I THINK SHE'LL LIKE IT.
THANK YOU, SHANKS!
THIS IS AMAZING. NOW, I BETTER WRAP THIS UP BEFORE MY SISTERS COME!
Tales of the Haunted Horseman
HUH, FOR A DUSTY OLD BOOK, IT SURE IS SLIPPERY!
SLIP
KAPLUMP
GASP! THE BOOK!
LORI, WE'RE HERE. SIGH.

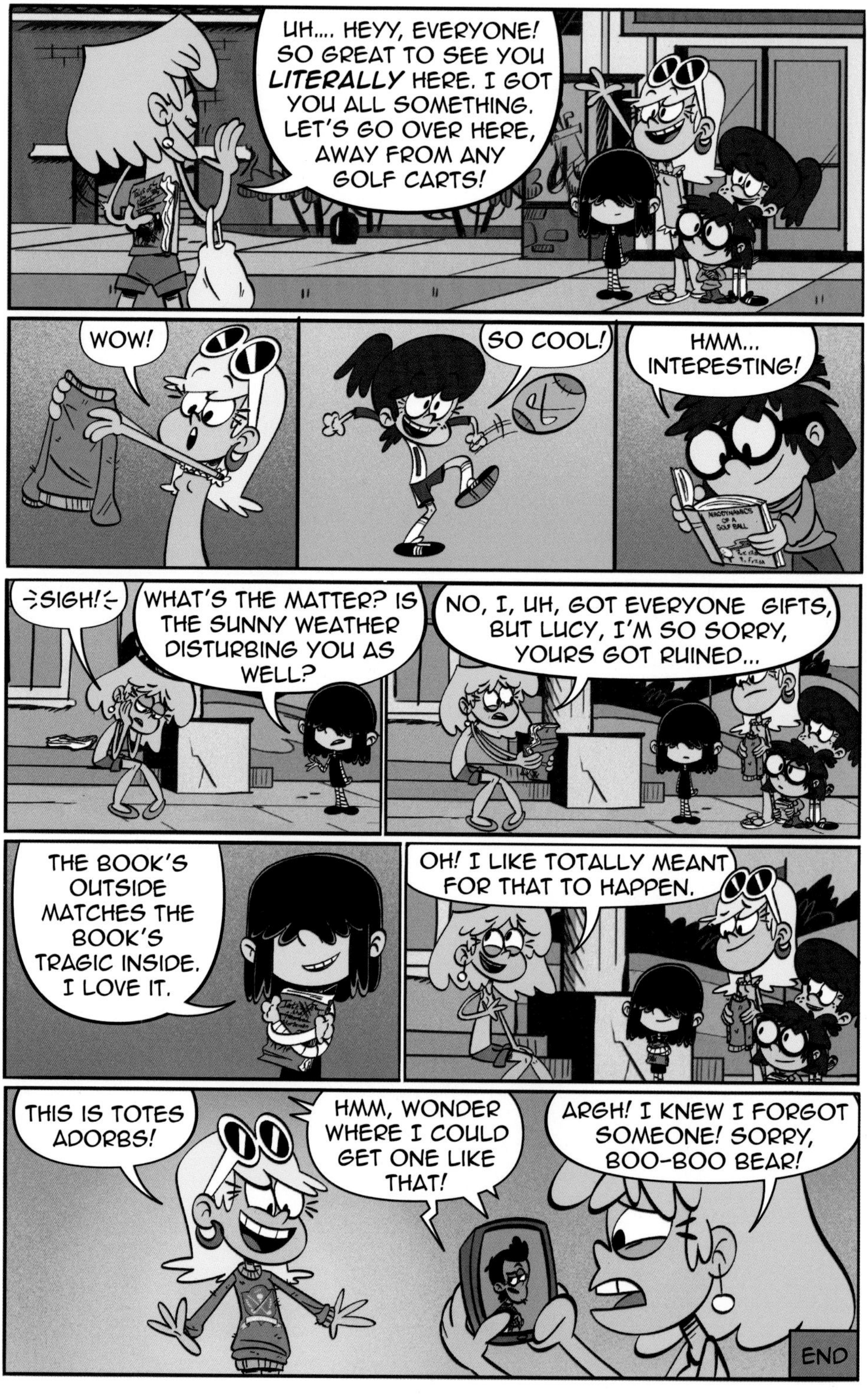

UH.... HEYY, EVERYONE! SO GREAT TO SEE YOU LITERALLY HERE. I GOT YOU ALL SOMETHING. LET'S GO OVER HERE, AWAY FROM ANY GOLF CARTS!
WOW!
SO COOL!
HMM... INTERESTING!
SIGH!
WHAT'S THE MATTER? IS THE SUNNY WEATHER DISTURBING YOU AS WELL?
NO, I, UH, GOT EVERYONE GIFTS, BUT LUCY, I'M SO SORRY, YOURS GOT RUINED...
THE BOOK'S OUTSIDE MATCHES THE BOOK'S TRAGIC INSIDE. I LOVE IT.
OH! I LIKE TOTALLY MEANT FOR THAT TO HAPPEN.
THIS IS TOTES ADORBS!
HMM, WONDER WHERE I COULD GET ONE LIKE THAT!
ARGH! I KNEW I FORGOT SOMEONE! SORRY, BOO-BOO BEAR!
END

"A FRUITLESS ENDEAVOR"

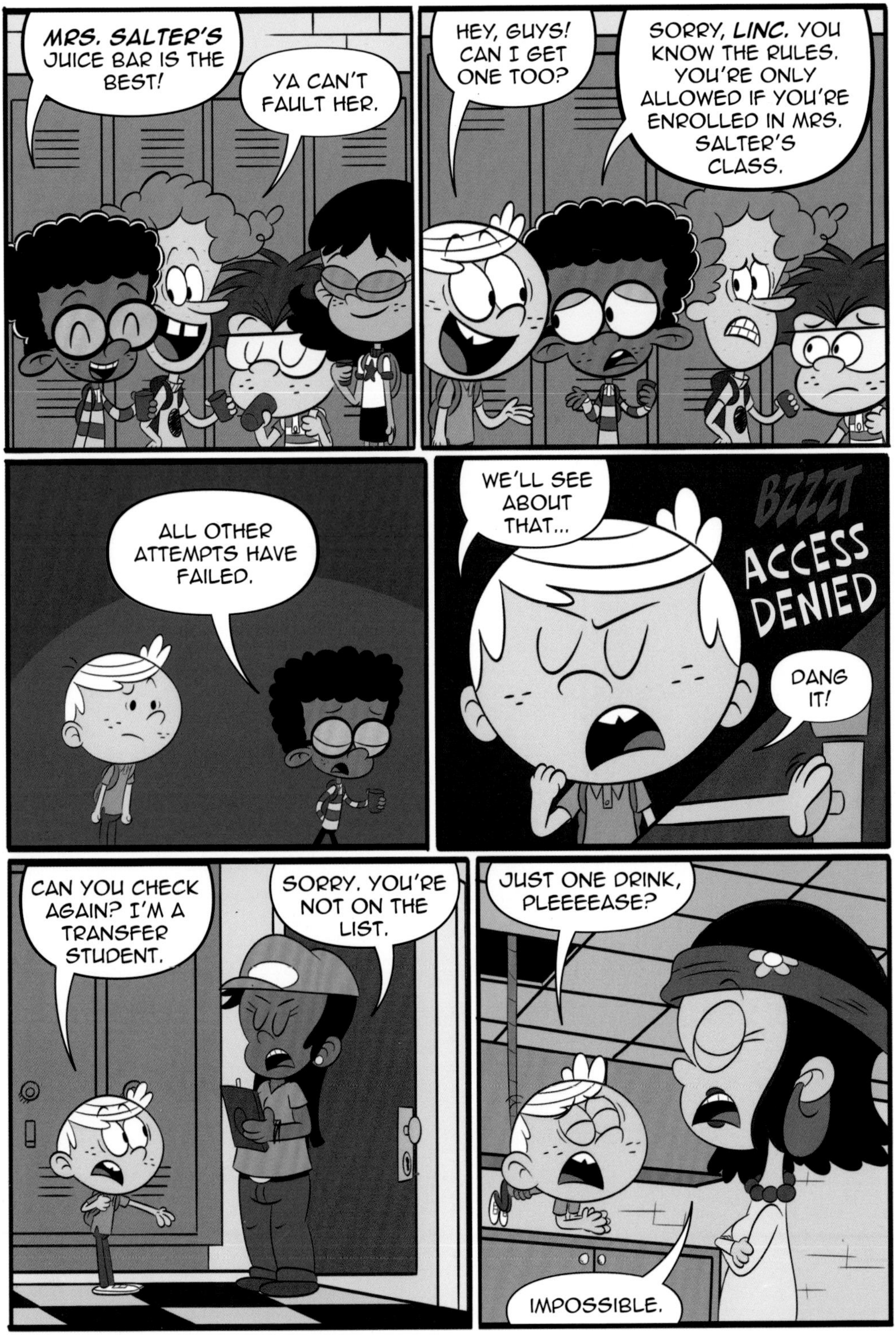
MRS. SALTER'S JUICE BAR IS THE BEST!
YA CAN'T FAULT HER.
HEY, GUYS! CAN I GET ONE TOO?
SORRY, LINC. YOU KNOW THE RULES. YOU'RE ONLY ALLOWED IF YOU'RE ENROLLED IN MRS. SALTER'S CLASS.
ALL OTHER ATTEMPTS HAVE FAILED.
WE'LL SEE ABOUT THAT...
BZZZT
ACCESS DENIED
DANG IT!
CAN YOU CHECK AGAIN? I'M A TRANSFER STUDENT.
SORRY. YOU'RE NOT ON THE LIST.
JUST ONE DRINK, PLEEEEASE?
IMPOSSIBLE.

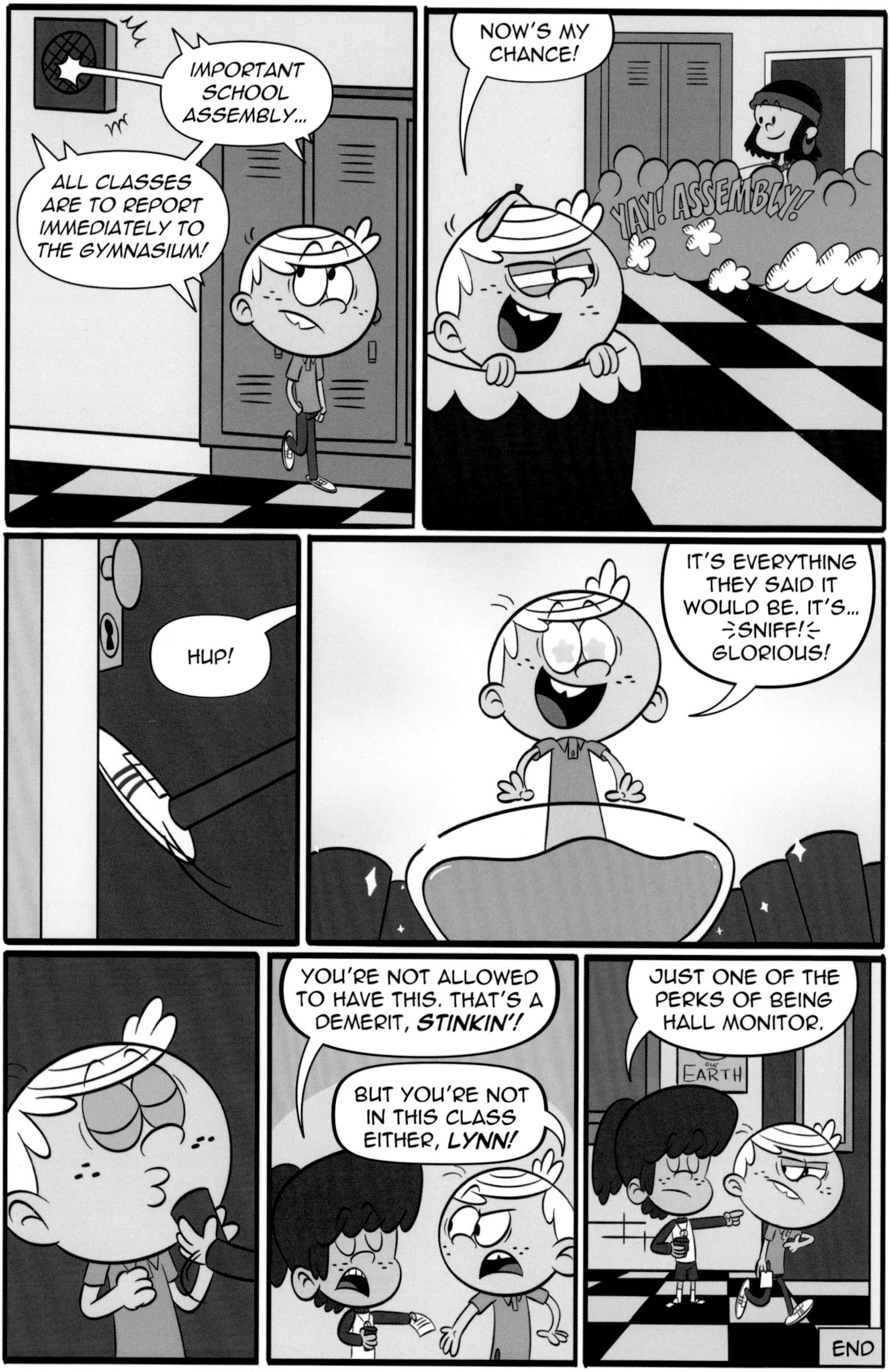
IMPORTANT SCHOOL ASSEMBLY...
ALL CLASSES ARE TO REPORT IMMEDIATELY TO THE GYMNASIUM!
NOW'S MY CHANCE!
YAY! ASSEMBLY!
HUP!
IT'S EVERYTHING THEY SAID IT WOULD BE. IT'S... SNIFF! GLORIOUS!
YOU'RE NOT ALLOWED TO HAVE THIS. THAT'S A DEMERIT, STINKIN'!
BUT YOU'RE NOT IN THIS CLASS EITHER, LYNN!
JUST ONE OF THE PERKS OF BEING HALL MONITOR.
EARTH
END

"SLEEPLESS IN PRESCHOOL"

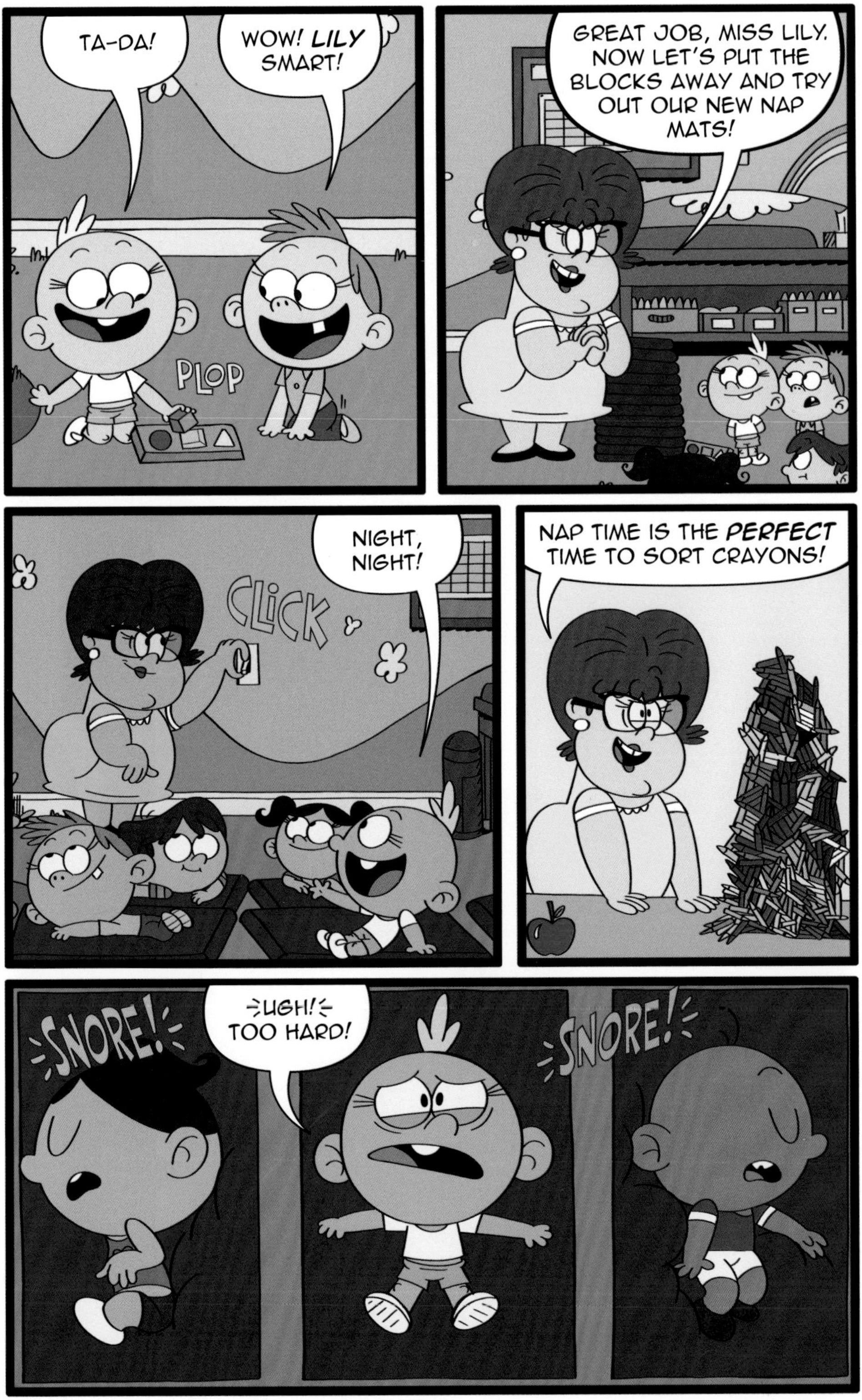

TA-DA!
WOW! *LILY* SMART!
PLOP
GREAT JOB, MISS LILY. NOW LET'S PUT THE BLOCKS AWAY AND TRY OUT OUR NEW NAP MATS!
CLICK
NIGHT, NIGHT!
NAP TIME IS THE *PERFECT* TIME TO SORT CRAYONS!
SNORE!
UGH! TOO HARD!
SNORE!

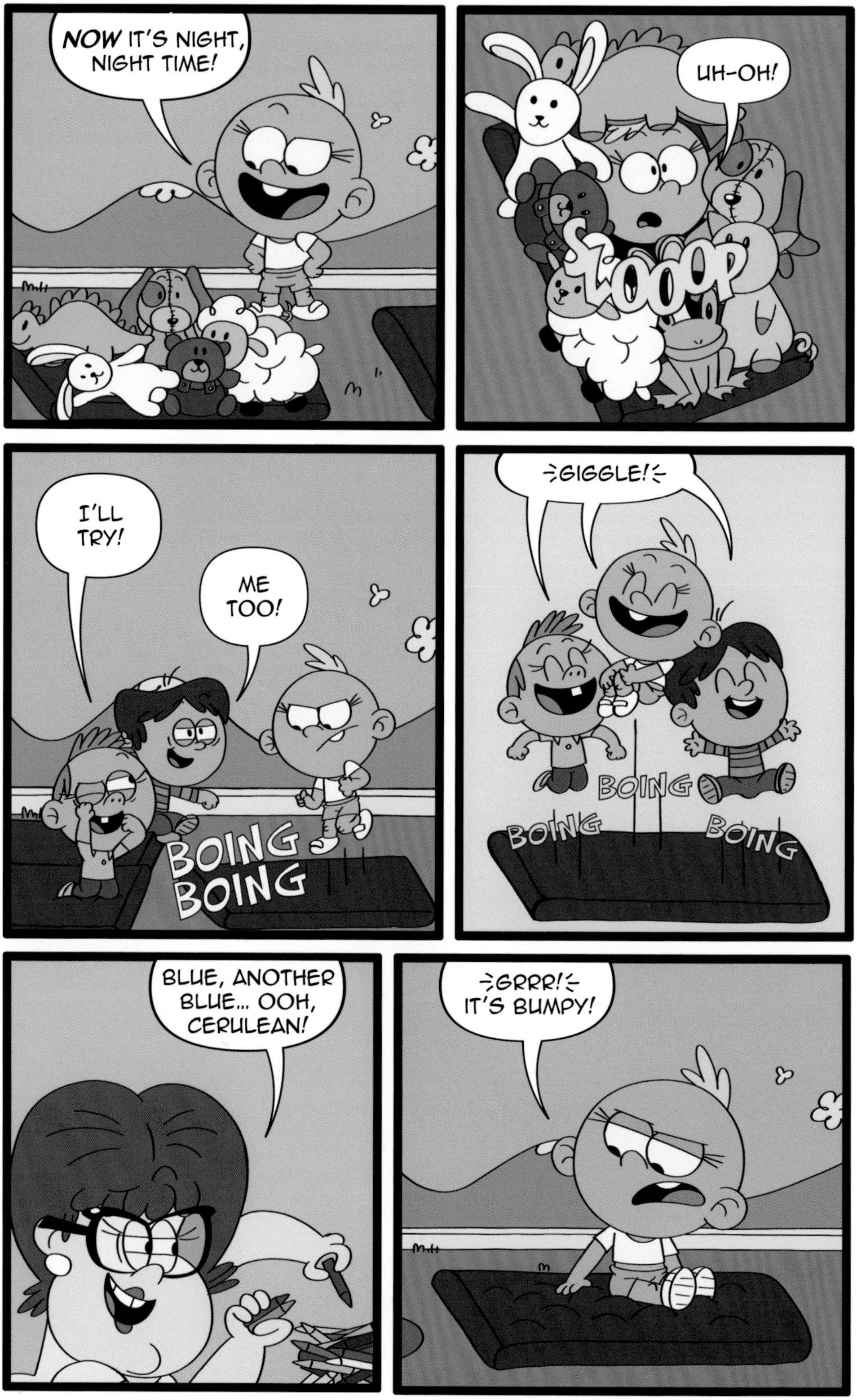
NOW IT'S NIGHT, NIGHT TIME!
UH-OH!
SZOOOP
I'LL TRY!
ME TOO!
BOING BOING
GIGGLE!
BOING BOING BOING
BLUE, ANOTHER BLUE... OOH, CERULEAN!
GRRR! IT'S BUMPY!

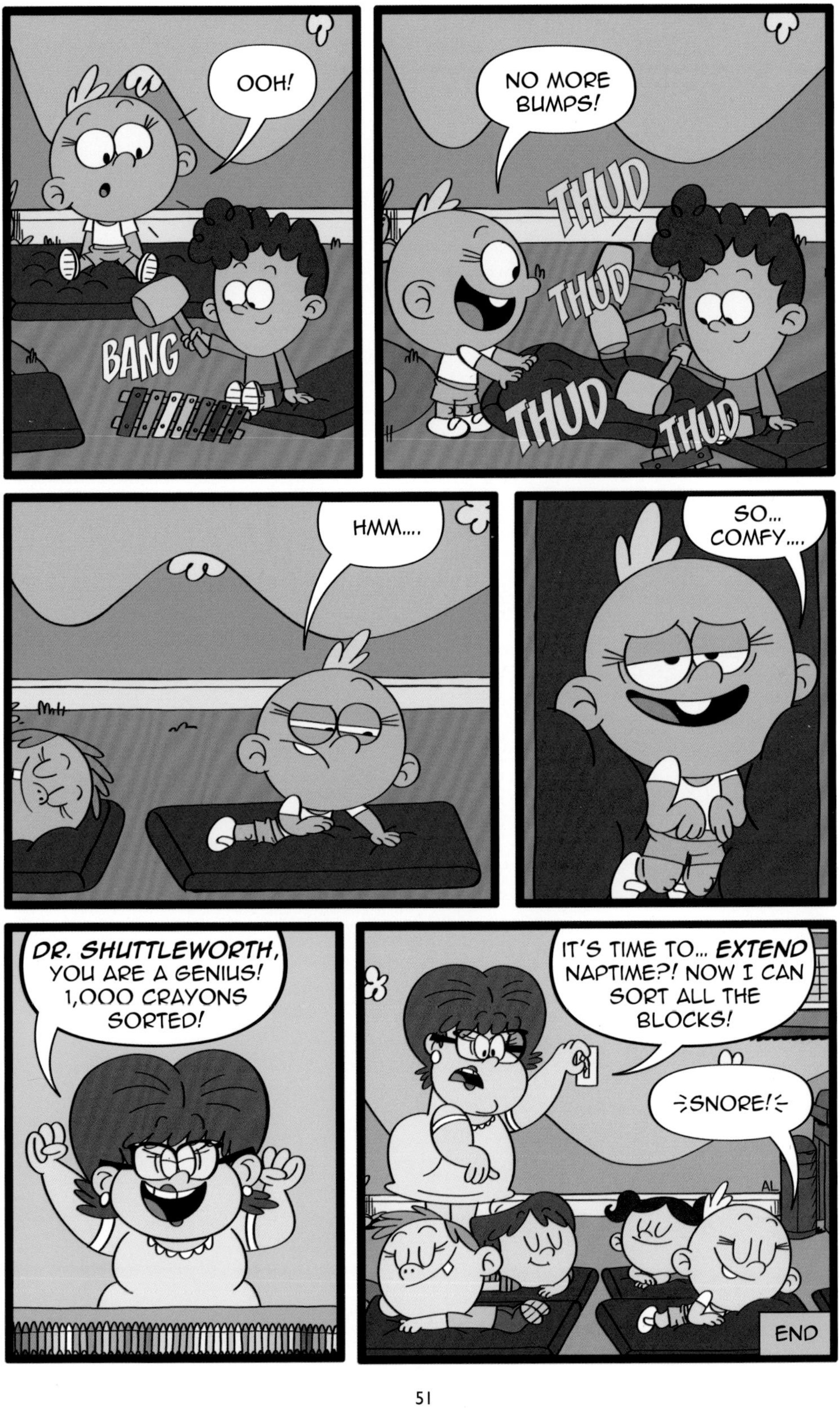
OOH!
BANG
NO MORE BUMPS!
THUD
THUD
THUD
THUD
HMM....
SO... COMFY....
DR. SHUTTLEWORTH, YOU ARE A GENIUS! 1,000 CRAYONS SORTED!
IT'S TIME TO... EXTEND NAPTIME?! NOW I CAN SORT ALL THE BLOCKS!
SNORE!
AL
END

"ALICE FORGIVEN"

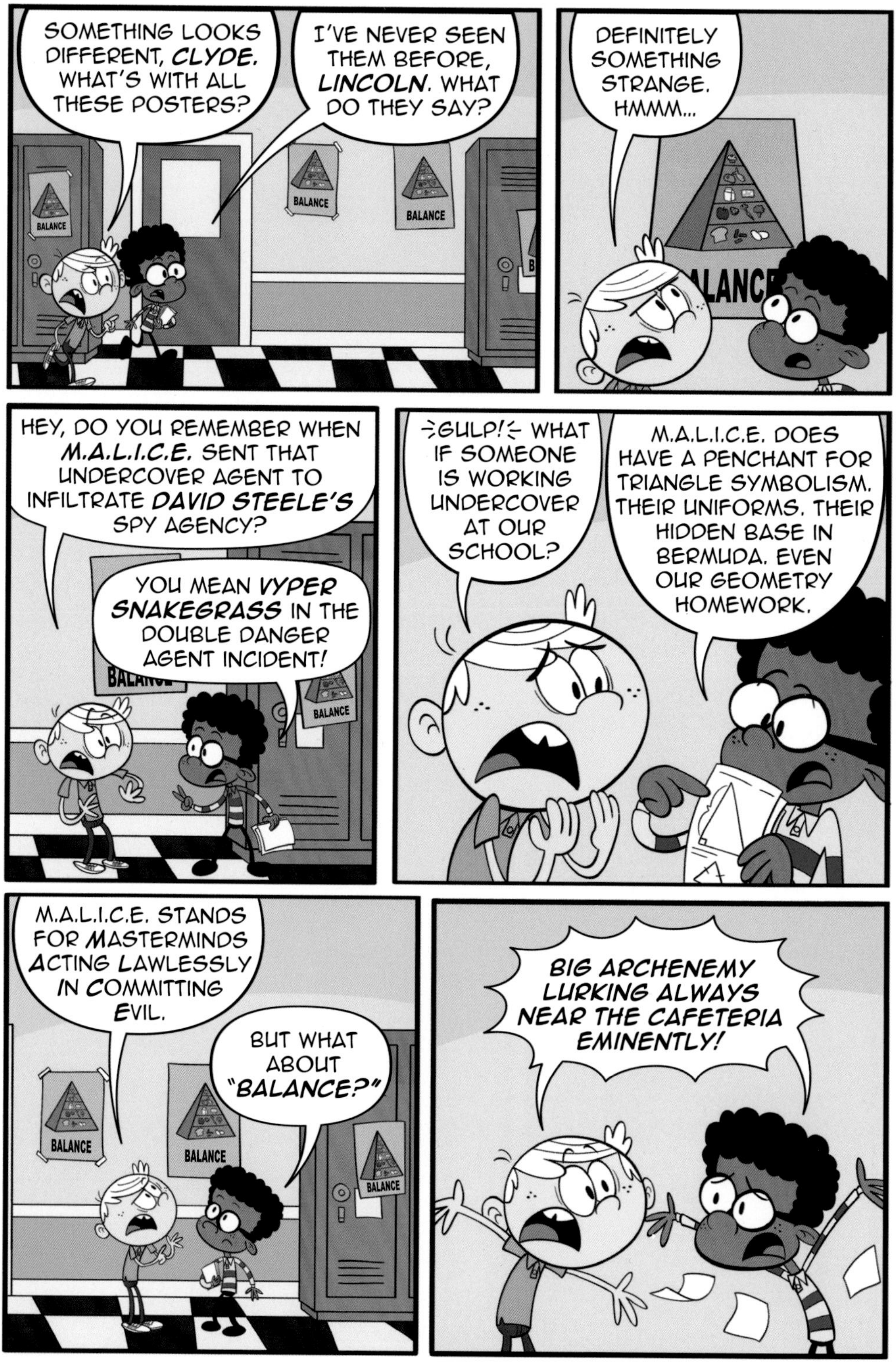

SOMETHING LOOKS DIFFERENT, CLYDE. WHAT'S WITH ALL THESE POSTERS?
I'VE NEVER SEEN THEM BEFORE, LINCOLN. WHAT DO THEY SAY?
BALANCE
DEFINITELY SOMETHING STRANGE. HMMM...
HEY, DO YOU REMEMBER WHEN M.A.L.I.C.E. SENT THAT UNDERCOVER AGENT TO INFILTRATE DAVID STEELE'S SPY AGENCY?
YOU MEAN VYPER SNAKEGRASS IN THE DOUBLE DANGER AGENT INCIDENT!
GULP! WHAT IF SOMEONE IS WORKING UNDERCOVER AT OUR SCHOOL?
M.A.L.I.C.E. DOES HAVE A PENCHANT FOR TRIANGLE SYMBOLISM. THEIR UNIFORMS. THEIR HIDDEN BASE IN BERMUDA. EVEN OUR GEOMETRY HOMEWORK.
M.A.L.I.C.E. STANDS FOR MASTERMINDS ACTING LAWLESSLY IN COMMITTING EVIL.
BUT WHAT ABOUT "BALANCE?"
BIG ARCHENEMY LURKING ALWAYS NEAR THE CAFETERIA EMINENTLY!

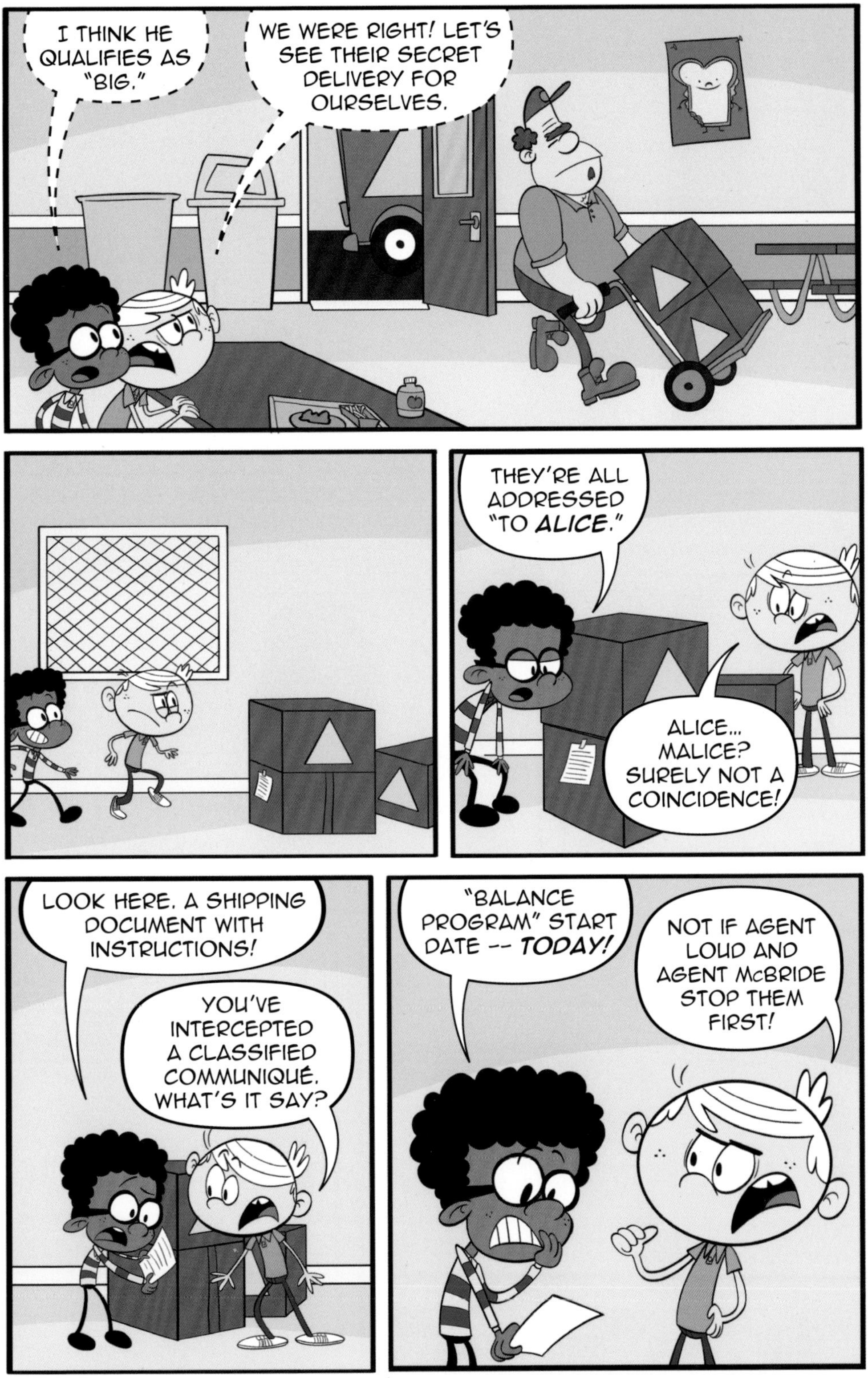
I THINK HE QUALIFIES AS "BIG."
WE WERE RIGHT! LET'S SEE THEIR SECRET DELIVERY FOR OURSELVES.
THEY'RE ALL ADDRESSED "TO ALICE."
ALICE... MALICE? SURELY NOT A COINCIDENCE!
LOOK HERE. A SHIPPING DOCUMENT WITH INSTRUCTIONS!
YOU'VE INTERCEPTED A CLASSIFIED COMMUNIQUÉ. WHAT'S IT SAY?
"BALANCE PROGRAM" START DATE -- TODAY!
NOT IF AGENT LOUD AND AGENT McBRIDE STOP THEM FIRST!

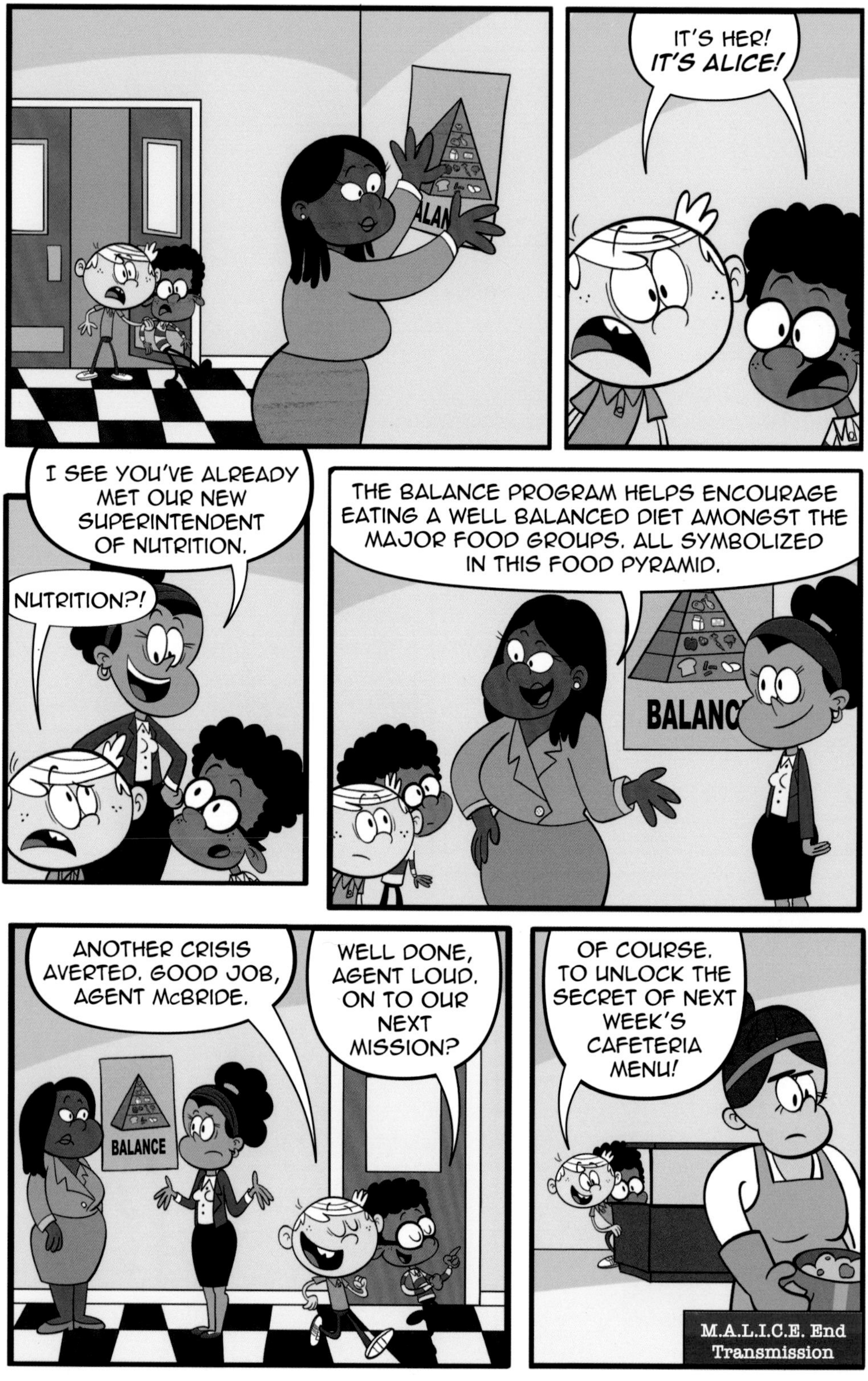
BALAN
IT'S HER!
IT'S ALICE!
I SEE YOU'VE ALREADY MET OUR NEW SUPERINTENDENT OF NUTRITION.
NUTRITION?!
THE BALANCE PROGRAM HELPS ENCOURAGE EATING A WELL BALANCED DIET AMONGST THE MAJOR FOOD GROUPS. ALL SYMBOLIZED IN THIS FOOD PYRAMID.
BALANC
ANOTHER CRISIS AVERTED. GOOD JOB, AGENT McBRIDE.
WELL DONE, AGENT LOUD. ON TO OUR NEXT MISSION?
BALANCE
OF COURSE. TO UNLOCK THE SECRET OF NEXT WEEK'S CAFETERIA MENU!
M.A.L.I.C.E. End Transmission

"INTERSTELLA"

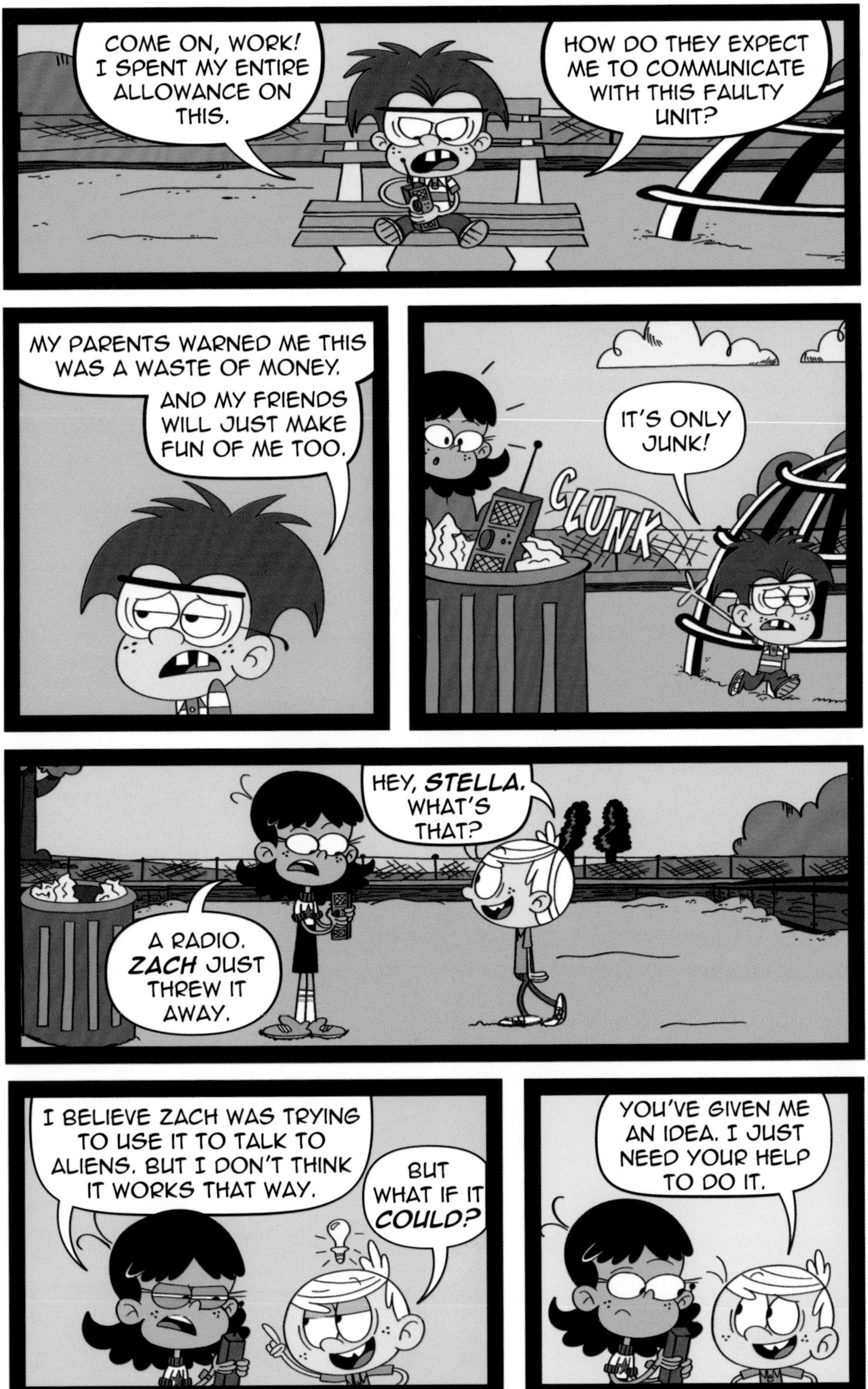

COME ON, WORK! I SPENT MY ENTIRE ALLOWANCE ON THIS.
HOW DO THEY EXPECT ME TO COMMUNICATE WITH THIS FAULTY UNIT?
MY PARENTS WARNED ME THIS WAS A WASTE OF MONEY.
AND MY FRIENDS WILL JUST MAKE FUN OF ME TOO.
IT'S ONLY JUNK!
CLUNK
HEY, STELLA. WHAT'S THAT?
A RADIO. ZACH JUST THREW IT AWAY.
I BELIEVE ZACH WAS TRYING TO USE IT TO TALK TO ALIENS. BUT I DON'T THINK IT WORKS THAT WAY.
BUT WHAT IF IT COULD?
YOU'VE GIVEN ME AN IDEA. I JUST NEED YOUR HELP TO DO IT.

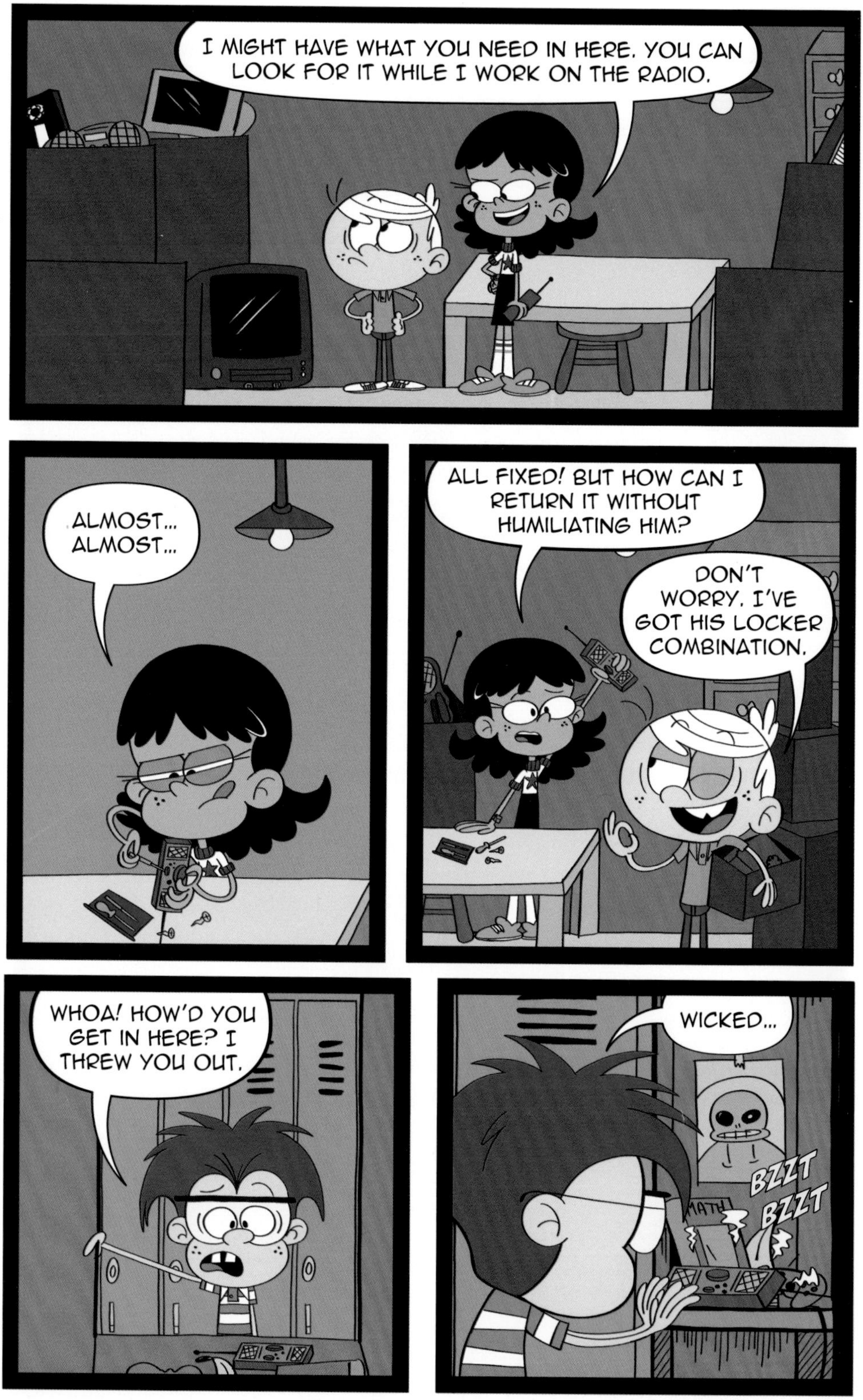
I MIGHT HAVE WHAT YOU NEED IN HERE. YOU CAN LOOK FOR IT WHILE I WORK ON THE RADIO.
ALMOST... ALMOST...
ALL FIXED! BUT HOW CAN I RETURN IT WITHOUT HUMILIATING HIM?
DON'T WORRY. I'VE GOT HIS LOCKER COMBINATION.
WHOA! HOW'D YOU GET IN HERE? I THREW YOU OUT.
WICKED...
MATH
BZZT BZZT

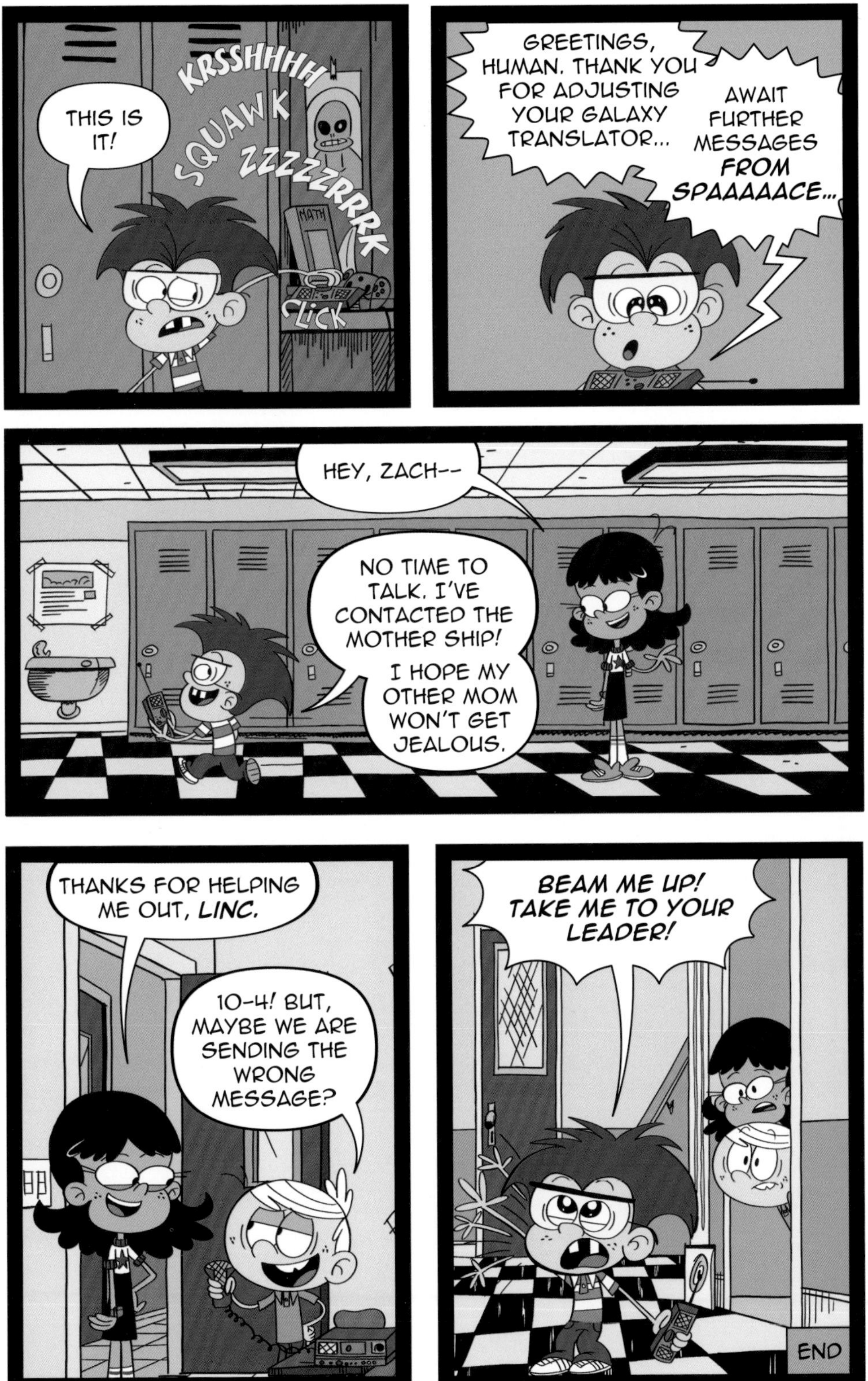
THIS IS IT!
KRSSHHHH!
SQUAWK
ZZZZZRRRK
MATH
CLICK
GREETINGS, HUMAN. THANK YOU FOR ADJUSTING YOUR GALAXY TRANSLATOR...
AWAIT FURTHER MESSAGES *FROM SPAAAAACE...*
HEY, ZACH--
NO TIME TO TALK. I'VE CONTACTED THE MOTHER SHIP!
I HOPE MY OTHER MOM WON'T GET JEALOUS.
THANKS FOR HELPING ME OUT, *LINC.*
10-4! BUT, MAYBE WE ARE SENDING THE WRONG MESSAGE?
BEAM ME UP! TAKE ME TO YOUR LEADER!
END

"THE TEACHERS LOUNGE"

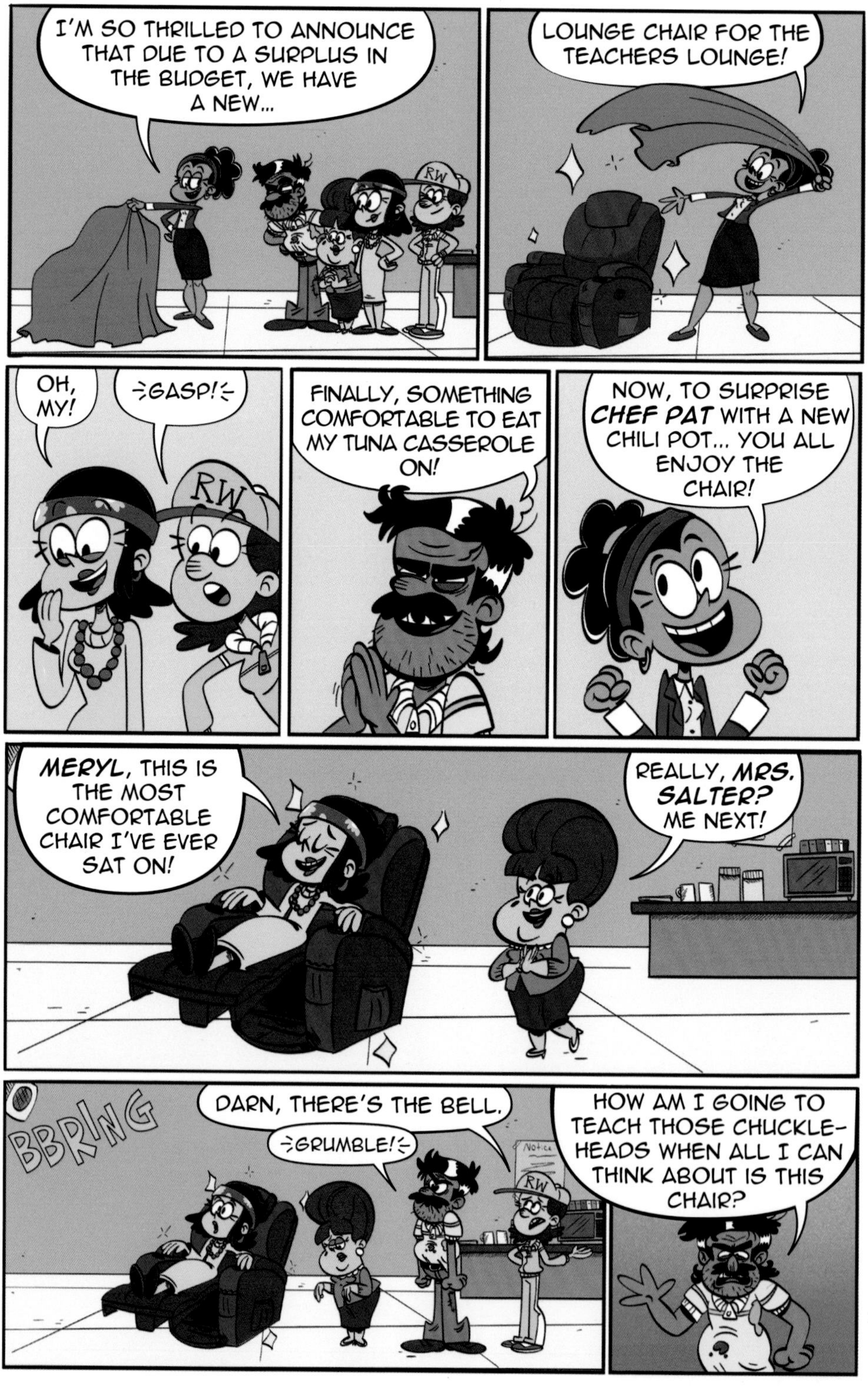
I'M SO THRILLED TO ANNOUNCE THAT DUE TO A SURPLUS IN THE BUDGET, WE HAVE A NEW...
RW
LOUNGE CHAIR FOR THE TEACHERS LOUNGE!
OH, MY!
GASP!
RW
FINALLY, SOMETHING COMFORTABLE TO EAT MY TUNA CASSEROLE ON!
NOW, TO SURPRISE CHEF PAT WITH A NEW CHILI POT... YOU ALL ENJOY THE CHAIR!
MERYL, THIS IS THE MOST COMFORTABLE CHAIR I'VE EVER SAT ON!
REALLY, MRS. SALTER? ME NEXT!
BBRING
DARN, THERE'S THE BELL.
GRUMBLE!
RW
HOW AM I GOING TO TEACH THOSE CHUCKLE-HEADS WHEN ALL I CAN THINK ABOUT IS THIS CHAIR?

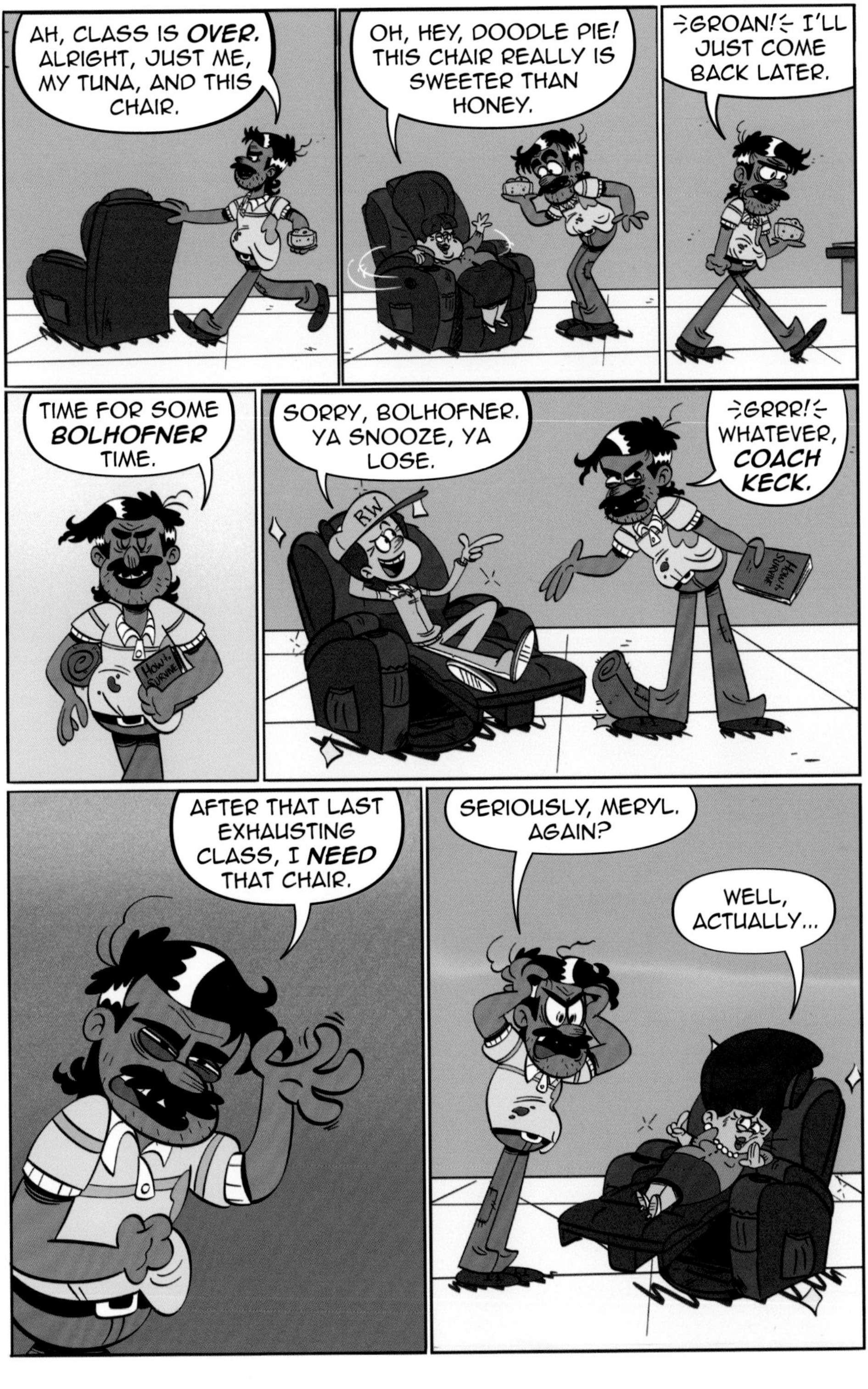
AH, CLASS IS **OVER.** ALRIGHT, JUST ME, MY TUNA, AND THIS CHAIR.
OH, HEY, DOODLE PIE! THIS CHAIR REALLY IS SWEETER THAN HONEY.
GROAN! I'LL JUST COME BACK LATER.
TIME FOR SOME **BOLHOFNER** TIME.
SORRY, BOLHOFNER. YA SNOOZE, YA LOSE.
GRRR! WHATEVER, **COACH KECK.**
AFTER THAT LAST EXHAUSTING CLASS, I **NEED** THAT CHAIR.
SERIOUSLY, MERYL. AGAIN?
WELL, ACTUALLY...

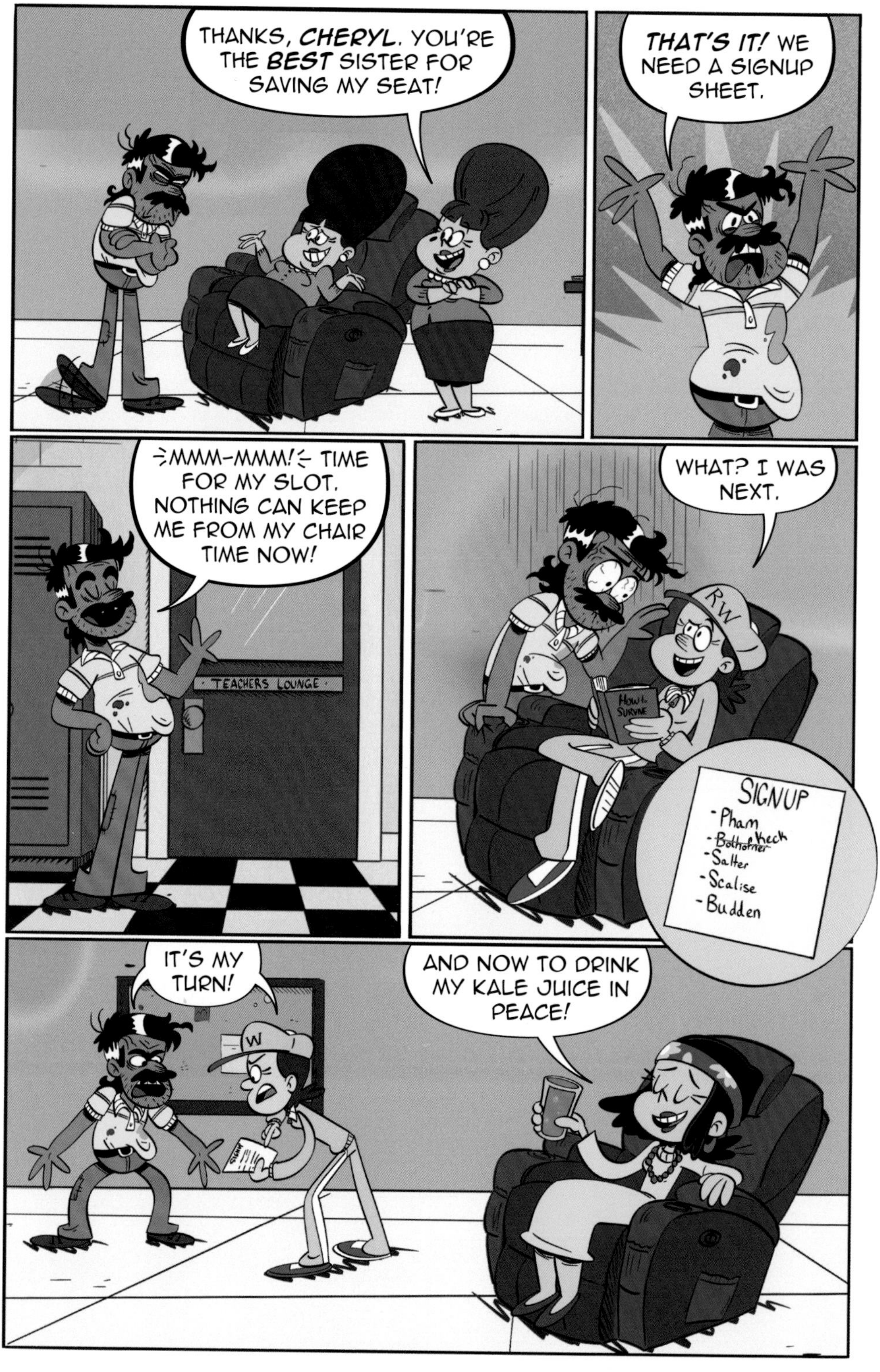
THANKS, CHERYL. YOU'RE THE BEST SISTER FOR SAVING MY SEAT!
THAT'S IT! WE NEED A SIGNUP SHEET.
MMM-MMM! TIME FOR MY SLOT. NOTHING CAN KEEP ME FROM MY CHAIR TIME NOW!
TEACHERS LOUNGE
WHAT? I WAS NEXT.
SIGNUP
-Pham
-Bothofner Heck
-Salter
-Scalise
-Budden
IT'S MY TURN!
AND NOW TO DRINK MY KALE JUICE IN PEACE!

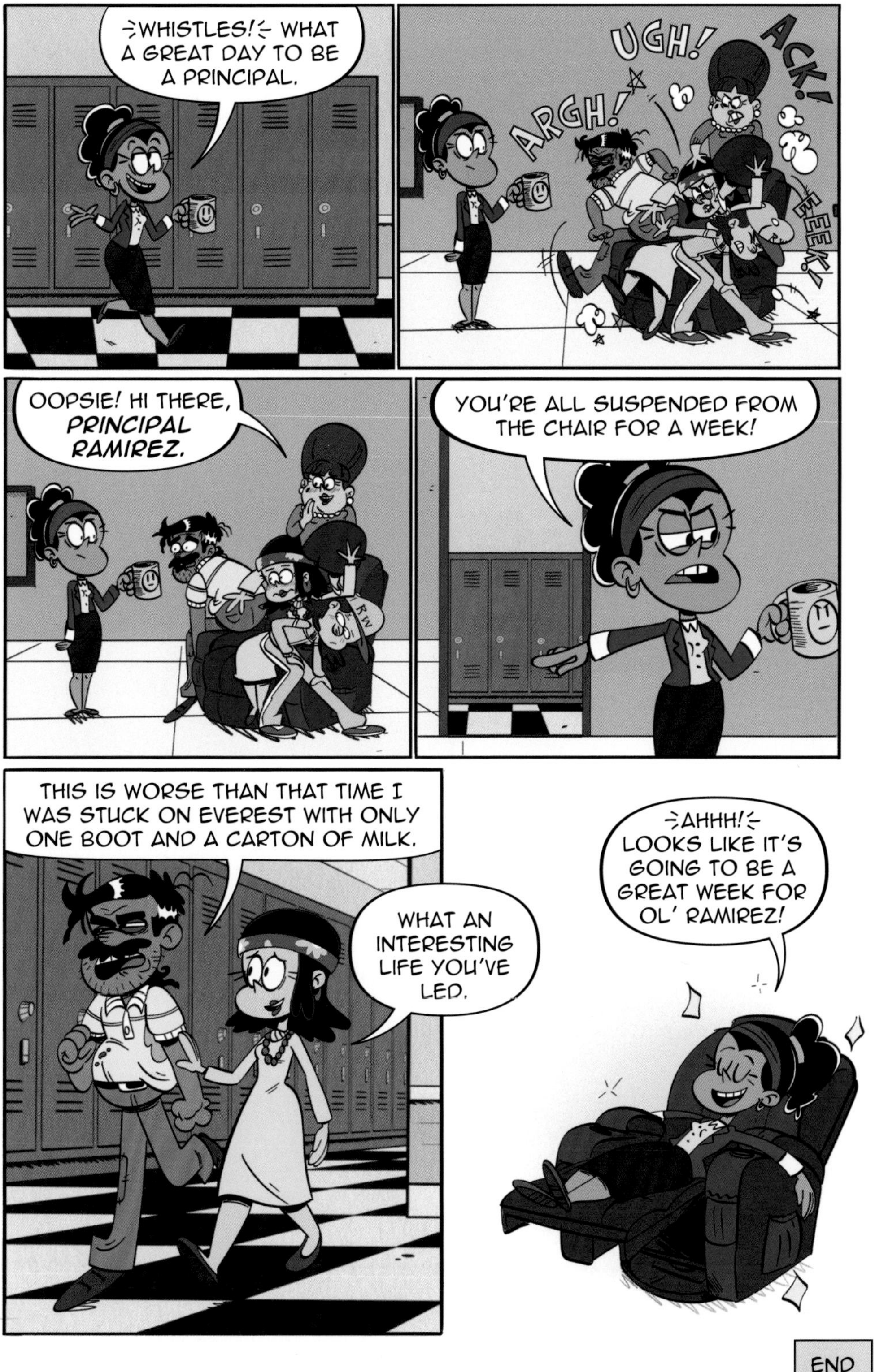

WHISTLES! WHAT A GREAT DAY TO BE A PRINCIPAL.
UGH!
ACK!
ARGH!
EEEK!
OOPSIE! HI THERE, PRINCIPAL RAMIREZ.
YOU'RE ALL SUSPENDED FROM THE CHAIR FOR A WEEK!
THIS IS WORSE THAN THAT TIME I WAS STUCK ON EVEREST WITH ONLY ONE BOOT AND A CARTON OF MILK.
WHAT AN INTERESTING LIFE YOU'VE LED.
AHHH! LOOKS LIKE IT'S GOING TO BE A GREAT WEEK FOR OL' RAMIREZ!
END

nickelodeon GRAPHIC NOVELS AVAILABLE FROM PAPERCUTZ

THE LOUD HOUSE
THERE WILL BE CHAOS

THE LOUD HOUSE
#1
"There Will Be Chaos"

THE LOUD HOUSE

THE LOUD HOUSE
#2
"There Will Be More Chaos"

THE LOUD HOUSE
LIVE LIFE LOUD!

THE LOUD HOUSE
#3
"Live Life Loud!"

THE LOUD HOUSE
FAMILY TREE
KEEP OUT!

THE LOUD HOUSE
#4
"Family Tree"

THE LOUD HOUSE
AFTER DARK

THE LOUD HOUSE
#5
"After Dark"

THE LOUD HOUSE
LOUD & PROUD

THE LOUD HOUSE
#6
"Loud & Proud"

THE LOUD HOUSE
THE STRUGGLE IS REAL

THE LOUD HOUSE
#7
"The Struggle is Real"

THE LOUD HOUSE
Livin' La Casa Loud!

THE LOUD HOUSE
#8
"Livin' La Casa Loud!"

THE LOUD HOUSE
ULTIMATE HANGOUT

THE LOUD HOUSE
#9
"Ultimate Hangout"

THE LOUD HOUSE
THE MANY FACES OF LINCOLN LOUD

THE LOUD HOUSE
#10
"The Many Faces of Lincoln Loud"

THE LOUD HOUSE
WHO'S THE LOUDEST?

THE LOUD HOUSE
#11
"Who's the Loudest?"

THE LOUD HOUSE
THE CASE OF THE STOLEN DRAWERS

THE LOUD HOUSE
#12
"The Case of the Stolen Drawers"

THE LOUD HOUSE
LUCY ROLLS THE DICE

THE LOUD HOUSE
#13
"Lucy Rolls the Dice"

THE LOUD HOUSE
GUESSING GAMES

THE LOUD HOUSE
#14
"Guessing Games"

THE LOUD HOUSE
THE MISSING LINC

THE LOUD HOUSE
#15
"The Missing Linc"

COMING SOON

THE LOUD HOUSE
LOUD AND CLEAR

THE LOUD HOUSE
#16
"Loud and Clear"

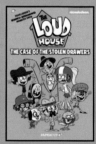

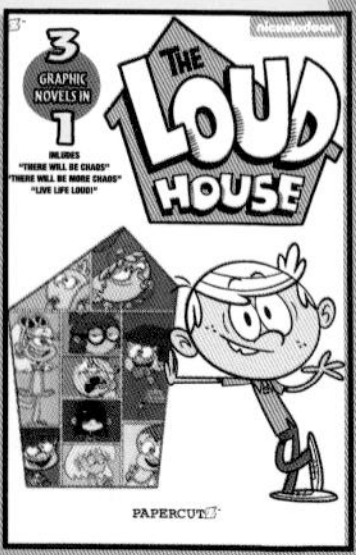
3 GRAPHIC NOVELS IN 1
THE LOUD HOUSE
PAPERCUTZ

THE LOUD HOUSE
3 IN 1
#1

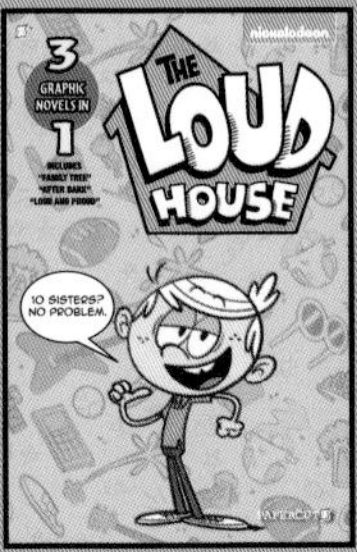
3 GRAPHIC NOVELS IN 1
THE LOUD HOUSE
10 SISTERS? NO PROBLEM.

THE LOUD HOUSE
3 IN 1
#2

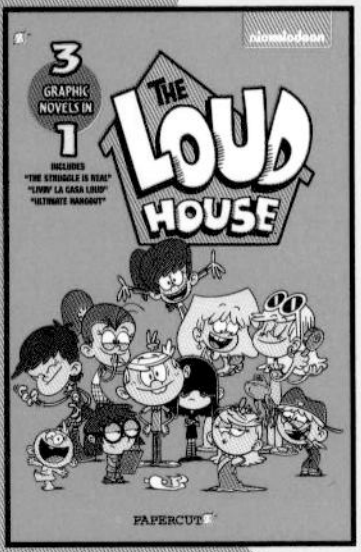
3 GRAPHIC NOVELS IN 1
THE LOUD HOUSE
PAPERCUTZ

THE LOUD HOUSE
3 IN 1
#3

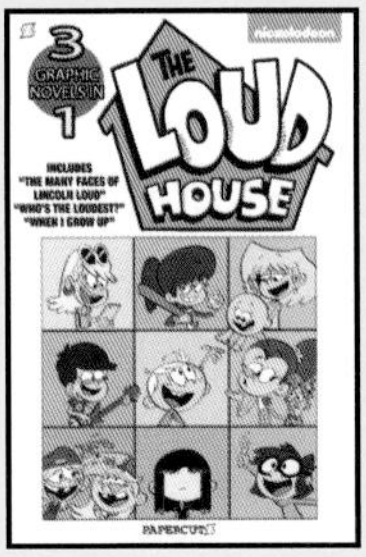
3 GRAPHIC NOVELS IN 1
THE LOUD HOUSE

THE LOUD HOUSE
3 IN 1
#4

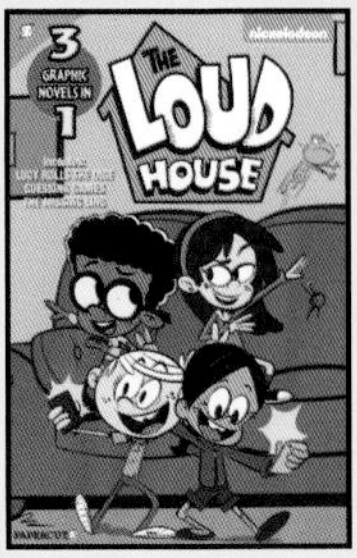
3 GRAPHIC NOVELS IN 1
THE LOUD HOUSE

THE LOUD HOUSE
3 IN 1
#5

COMING SOON

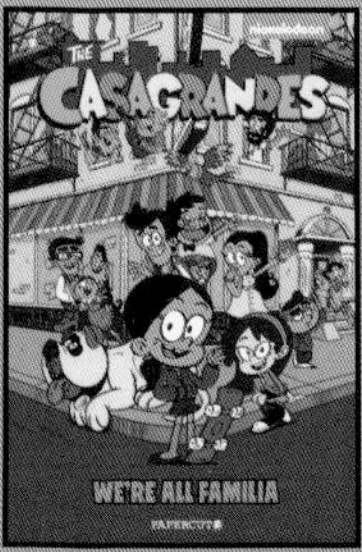
THE CASAGRANDES
WE'RE ALL FAMILIA
PAPERCUTZ

THE CASAGRANDES
#1
"We're All Familia"

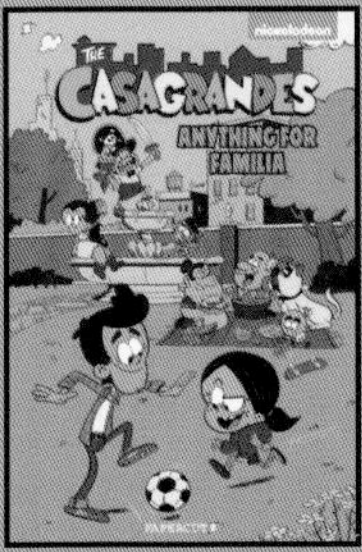
THE CASAGRANDES
ANYTHING FOR FAMILIA

THE CASAGRANDES
#2
"Anything for Familia"

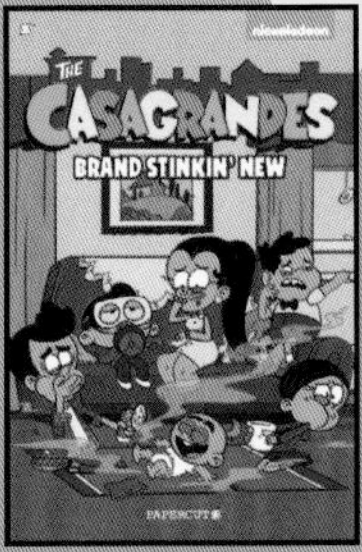
THE CASAGRANDES
BRAND STINKIN' NEW
PAPERCUTZ

THE CASAGRANDES
#3
"Brand Stinkin' New"

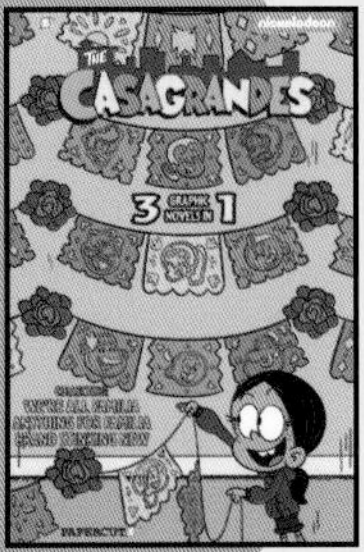
THE CASAGRANDES
3 GRAPHIC NOVELS IN 1

THE CASAGRANDES
3 IN 1
#1

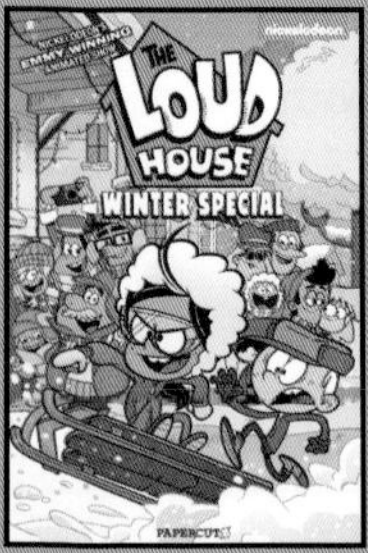
THE LOUD HOUSE
WINTER SPECIAL
PAPERCUTZ

THE LOUD HOUSE
WINTER SPECIAL

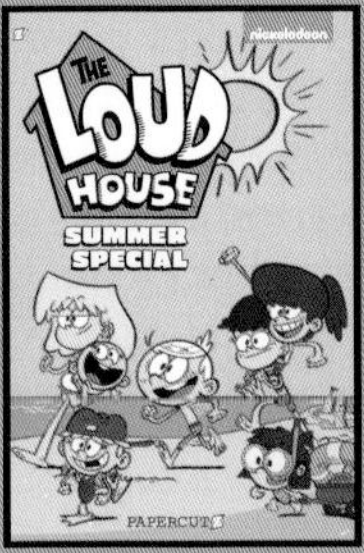
THE LOUD HOUSE
SUMMER SPECIAL
PAPERCUTZ

THE LOUD HOUSE
SUMMER SPECIAL

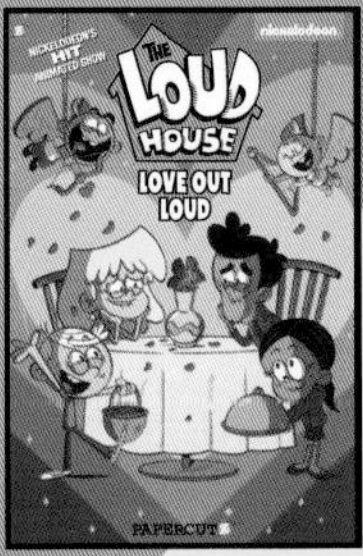
THE LOUD HOUSE
LOVE OUT LOUD
PAPERCUTZ

THE LOUD HOUSE
LOVE OUT LOUD
SPECIAL

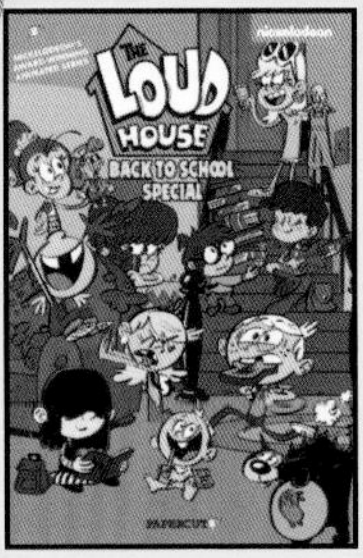
THE LOUD HOUSE
BACK TO SCHOOL SPECIAL
PAPERCUTZ

THE LOUD HOUSE
BACK TO SCHOOL
SPECIAL

THE LOUD HOUSE and THE CASAGRANDES graphic novels and specials are available for $7.99 each in paperback, $12.99 each in hardcover. THE LOUD HOUSE 3 IN 1 and THE CASAGRANDES 3 IN 1 graphic novels are available for $14.99 each in paperback only.

Available from booksellers everywhere. You can also order online from Papercutz.com, or call 1-800-886-1223, Monday through Friday, 9-5 EST. MC, Visa, and AmEx accepted. To order by mail, please add $5.00 for postage and handling for the first book ordered, $1.00 for each additional book and make check payable to NBM Publishing.
Send to: Papercutz, 160 Broadway, Suite 700, East Wing, New York, NY 10038.

The Loud House and The Casagrandes graphic novels are also available digitally wherever e-books are sold.

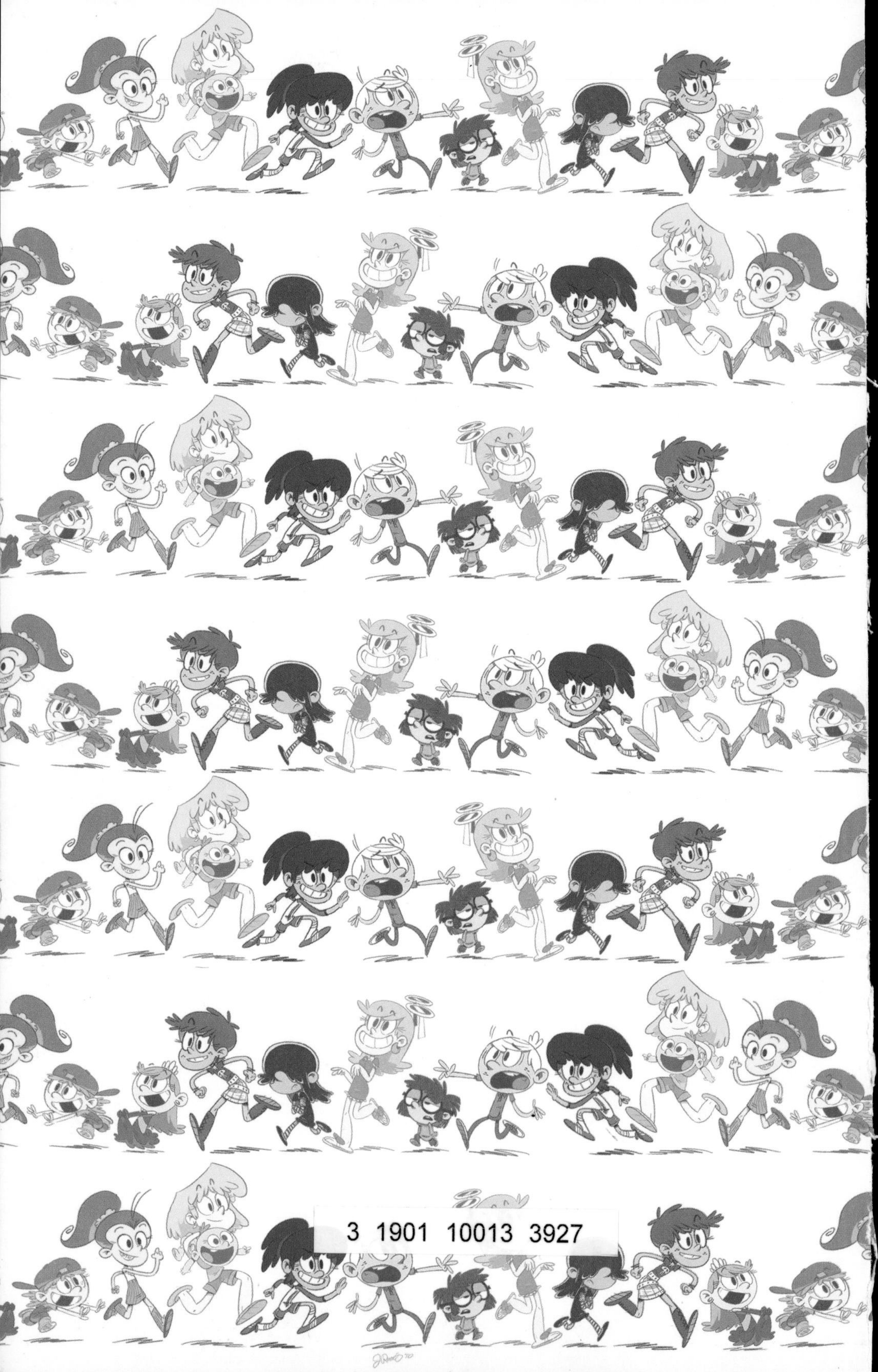